SHADOW PASTORS

Sacred Scars and Musings of a
Calling Interrupted

SHADOW PASTORS
Sacred Scars and Musings of a Calling Interrupted

Dr. Sandra L. Barnes

Shadow Pastors
Copyright © 2021 by Sandra L. Barnes

Content Editor: Alexandra Crawford
Copy Editor: Karen Slininger
Editor-in-Chief: Kristi King-Morgan
Formatting: Kristi King-Morgan
Cover Artist: Krystina Hamilton
Assistant Editor: Maddy Drake

Printed in the United States of America

ISBN-978-1-947381-49-0

www.dreamingbigpublications.com

*This book is dedicated to the many women who take on
the mantle of leader.*

PART I

Chapter 1:

St. John's Church and God's

MOB

Super Saint inched under pews, around the chancel, and across the pulpit of St. John's Community Church. Her tiny frame cruised its vast canvas as her voice echoed, "Have no fear saints or sinners. I have come to save the day!" The young girl draped a purple and gold cape, actually a Sunbeam Choir robe, tightly around her bony shoulders to provide just the right buoyancy to scamper atop wooden surfaces without slipping. A silver-plated offering tray and a makeshift helmet completed the crime fighter's ensemble. After donning her superhero attire, she was certain no one could recognize the unassuming Marnie Hunter — daughter of St. John's leader, Pastor Lee Hunter, and his wife Evangelist Shannon Hunter. Marnie was undaunted in her dual quest to fight for justice and thwart evil. "I have taken a secret oath to fight against the principalities, powers, rulers of the world, and spiritual wickedness in high places." She mumbled certain words from the memorized portion of her father's sermons. Although only six years old, Marnie was trying to do her part to make the world safer and better.

"You can come with me today as long as you aren't underfoot." Her father shot a smirk Marnie's way.

"Aye okay!" The little girl quickly saluted. She worshipped those Saturdays with her father at St. John's even more than the sweet, cold treat they always got afterward that usually ended up trickling down her arm.

"Erected in 1824, did you know that St. John's is the oldest church in the city?" Pastor Hunter regaled the historic congregation to anyone who would listen, including Marnie. Deep red enveloped the sanctuary, including the carpet, pew backs and seat pads, draperies, and even the prayer stands. The well-maintained but worn furniture in the sanctuary was sturdy enough for a tiny superhero's antics! An oak lectern loomed large at its center, adorned with an image of a cross and Christ's figure that was almost as tall as Marnie. The silver organ pipes were also sure to respond to the accompanist's lithe fingers with "What a Friend We Have in Jesus". Just as every piece of furniture in the sanctuary directed one's eye toward that cross, every aspect of worship liturgically pointed to Pastor Hunter's sermons. "Daddy, why can only men go into the pulpit? Why do women and children have to speak from the smaller stand next to the pulpit?" Her brow furrowed.

"Things are changing," his voice trailed. Yet on those Saturdays, the entire church belonged to Marnie!

Pastor Hunter typically went straight to his office in the rear of the building to practice his Sunday sermon, make weekly phone calls to elderly or shut-in members, counsel engaged couples, and complete the many tasks of an over-worked, underpaid full-time pastor. "Marnie, please promise to play quietly and don't go outside those sanctuary doors."

She rolled her eyes. Why would she want to leave the building when there were so many exciting adventures inside? For it was in that building that Super Saint came to life. On that particular Saturday, her imagination ran wild when she heard the faint moans, gurgles, grunts, and sighs coming from the recesses of the church basement that smelled of musky robes, holiday costumes, and history. Someone needed Super Saint's help!

As Marnie tiptoed toward the sound's origins, her initial excitement to aid the defenseless and defeat the demonic ebbed as she coldly considered what she might find. *Maybe I should go get Dad*, she mused. *No!* Heaven had endowed Super Saint with powers; she was undaunted. God was on her side. As she moved toward its epicenter, the noises steadily grew in strength, tenor, as well as clarity, and then echoed, drawing the inquisitive girl into the choir practice room at the rear of the basement.

As Marnie's eyes acclimated to the darkness, she stretched her lanky body forward far enough to see Sister Bethany White leaning against the back wall of the room. Marnie noticed the assistant choir director hastily enter the church earlier, but her presence was quickly forgotten amidst a particularly arduous crime-fighting spree. She trembled in fear as she saw Sister White's closed eyes, contorted face, and ridged posture. She seemed impaled against the wall. Then Marnie noticed a roundish mound moving up from the woman's midsection. Marnie gasped silently. It was just like the scene from that movie when the alien forced itself from its victim's stomach!

"I'll save you, Sister White!" Marnie was about to call out. She was about to bolt toward the well-loved choral leader when she realized that the gyrating mound wasn't a hell spawn, but the head of Minister Brandon Peters, the choir director! Marnie recognized his receding hairline and the semi-circular, curly brownish mat above his neck. Sister White lodged Minister Peters' head firmly between her legs. She also secured its location using all four of her limbs. Then Minister Peters' hands gradually moved up her body to rest on Sister White's breasts. Both of the choral leaders were rasping while attempting to muffle their throaty groans.

Marnie initially froze. She wasn't sure what she was witnessing, but somehow surmised that the act, location, and the hushed, intense responses meant that Super Saint wasn't needed after all. She slowly backed out of the shadowy room without disturbing either occupant. Moreover, she pushed the thought of telling her father from her mind. Nor would she tell their spouses. Her superpower of discernment meant that Marnie never told a soul what she saw that day.

Now, almost two decades later, Marnie was sitting across from the two adults who had unwittingly provided her first exposure to sex, secrecy, and shame. For better or worse, that clandestine tryst influenced her views and behavior toward sex. She wondered how long the worship leaders clandestinely met. Did they continue after that day? Did Jana Peters ever discover her husband's indiscretions, or did he end the affair after learning about his wife's breast cancer? Was this pre-choral coitus responsible for the death of both of Sister White's marriages? Now that they were both romantically available, Marnie wondered whether the two were a couple. She doubted it. The everyday experiences of love and relationships were seldom as exciting as the allure of fleeting encounters so passionately portrayed in movies. However, one thing was certain, although a bit grayer and rounder, both leaders were still committed to St. John's Church.

Marnie dragged her thoughts to the present because her father and about twenty other community leaders were about to meet to discuss the citywide Family and Friends Festival. Monthly meetings to prepare for the event were taking place at St. John's. As the Associate Minister of the neighboring Bethlehem Church, Marnie Hunter was her church's representative on the Interfaith Council and co-chairperson of the Festival Organizing Committee. Her pastor, Rev. Daniel Donaldson, delegated this administrative task to Marnie, one of her many responsibilities as "second in command" at Bethlehem. He often joked, "Minister Marnie, your faithful commitment to your duties enable me to faithfully commit to mine." Marnie believed he appreciated her hard work, but sometimes she felt that Pastor Donaldson took advantage of that commitment. Yet she relished any excuse to visit her old religious stomping ground and her father. The crevices and caverns of the old church renewed her spirit. She missed their Saturdays together and the adventures of Super Saint. Now they needed to get down to business!

"Let's please call this meeting to order." Mother Agnes Bonner looked over her gold-rimmed glasses at the group of ministers, lay leaders, and city volunteers. Some of the community leaders are new and did not know Mother Bonner. "As the chairperson of the festival committee, I am responsible for ensuring that the event appropriately represents God's House in the community." Marnie shivered. She continued, "For the last five years, the Beautification Committee has successfully organized these festivities. I am excited to present our plans for this summer's event!" Her small frame swayed like a sturdy rowboat buffeted against the wind.

Mother Bonner lifted her chin slightly as she described her numerous ecclesiastical hats. Although her husband established a national reputation for preaching and teaching, everyone knew that it was Mother Bonner who "got things done." Moreover, when she talked, you listened. Her administrative skills, moxie, and fervor gave her almost celebrity status. Mother Bonner made up for her slight stature with a voluminous voice and she had a stronghold on the festival plans. However, there were some concerns among younger committee members and last year's attendees about the Family and Friends Festival. It only celebrated certain families and wasn't friendly to certain folks.

Still Pastor Hunter asked Mother Bonner and her team to spearhead this year's planning. "Yes, Mother Bonner can be a bit domineering and set in her ways." Pastor Hunter avoided Marnie's eyes when they talked about the committee's composition. "Her commitment will ensure that things are done decently and in order. Moreover, with *you* as committee co-chairperson, I know that the festival will be more inclusive and diverse than last year's. Sometimes you have to deal with a few thorns to experience the beauty of a rose."

Yeah right, Marnie thought. She understood his message loud and clear. However, Marnie also wished older people would find new idioms to justify their decisions.

As the meeting proceeded, the young cleric felt her temperature gradually rise as she awaited what would surely be a political-laden experience. As Marnie unconsciously did during duress or conflict, she rubbed the linear swatches of coffee-colored scars that ran the length of the back of both her arms between her elbows and wrists. She always wore long sleeved shirts or blouses, even in humid weather. Few people saw her arms; most attributed her demur attire to ministerial protocol. Marnie was constantly reminded of their presence... and origin.

"There is so much to do, but we can do it. God is on our side. Our past festivals have been excellent! It may be difficult to surpass them, but we can certainly try." Mother Bonner leisurely removed the color-blocked linen shawl that matched her gray pin-striped suit and spectator shoes, signaling that it was time to get down to business! "I have taken the liberty to compile a list of proposed activities to consider. Please refer to page two." The ten-page novella included details for each activity - down to expected attire! Mother Bonner was nothing if not thorough. Marnie chuckled. The crackle of turning pages provided background noise for her directives.

"Excuse me, Mother Bonner," Minister Janice Cooper cautiously chimed. "God bless you for your continued commitment to both this community and this event. From our last meeting, I thought we were to reflect upon the strengths and areas for possible improvement over last year's festival and bring ideas to this brainstorming session?" Minister Cooper was a young cleric at a nearby church and a relatively new committee member. She realized the unstated pecking order and that she was at the bottom of it, yet dedication to community service fueled her remarks.

Mother Bonner's left brow raised. "*Janice*, I appreciate your thoughtful remarks. I am just trying to maximize our time together. I believe you're new to the committee *and* to ministry?" The younger woman's lips turned downward. The use of designated titles such as doctor, reverend, rabbi, pastor, bishop, evangelist, elder, imam, or deacon might seem trivial to outsiders, but were essential during inter-denominational, multi-cultural gatherings. Minister Cooper positioned her body for a confrontation. Mother Bonner's allies pursed their plum-colored lips and darted their eyes back and forth between the two women. If Marnie didn't intervene, all hell would break loose!

"Thank you, Mother Bonner, for your insight. We all appreciate your unwavering commitment to this annual endeavor and to the entire city," Marnie embellished a tad. "It wouldn't be a success every year without your input and involvement." That part was true. "As associate chairperson, might I suggest that, after a brief update by you, we brainstorm about ways to incorporate the best of past activities with new ideas." Marnie shifted her body toward the neophyte

16

cleric. "*Minister Cooper*, you had some great suggestions to attract younger people using social media. I personally wouldn't know how to tweet to save my life! I would love to learn how to attract and retain this scarce demographic."

Minister Cooper beamed. "Yes. Yes." Mother Bonner grudgingly nodded. Other committee members, old and young, smiled and began to chime in. Marnie continued to act as a buffer during the remainder of the meeting. She could see her father's toothy grin in the back of the room. She squelched the MOB, or *Mean Old Biddies*, if only for a short time.

"No one would ever convince those biddies that their bravado, mannerisms, and manners (or lack of) might not be Christ-like." Marnie's eyes rolled. "The Holy Spirit indwells every fiber of their beings or so they think." She smirked. "During the second Coming, God will surely head straight for them, whether they are above or below ground!" Pastor Hunter silently rubbed his daughter's taut shoulders as she vented.

At St. John's Church, most people deferred to the MOB's demands. However, when younger adults got together outside the purview of *the saints*, they described these older women using much more colorful ways — as MOBs. *It fits*, Marnie thought. Sometimes she felt ashamed for thinking about these elderly women so unflatteringly; most of the time she believed that they were well-intentioned. However, she also witnessed them squash persons like bugs who unwittingly threatened their beliefs and agendas.

MOBs existed at every church where Marnie served. These older women could quote scripture, content and address, at the drop of a hat. They knew the church's history ad nauseam and were long-standing members of every influential committee or ministry. Most importantly, they knew where all the bodies were buried. Most people obligingly deferred to MOBs because, truth be told, despite their abrasiveness, they were the unfailing workers, tithers, custodians, cooks, and keepers of sacred spaces. If Peter was the rock on which Christ built the Church, these women represented the proverbial mortar that held the masonry of the Church together. They pulled their weight and didn't mind letting you know it!

Marnie didn't lump all elderly Christian women together. For every MOB, there was a Sister Janis Jane. A broad shouldered, salt-and-pepper-haired mother, she always sat in *her* seat on the second pew to the right of the pulpit at Bethlehem Church, as she would kindly remind folks who mistakenly sat here. Unlike her peers who seemed to be trying to out "Amen" each other during worship service, Sister Jane sat composed, nodding slightly when Marnie preached. Once Marnie even asked her about her silent support. Above a whisper she replied, "Baby, I really don't want to hear any of the other ministers preach but the Pastor, but I *can* listen to you." Marnie beamed at the stoic curmudgeonly Christian. Marnie experienced MOBs more often than she cared to remember, but she wouldn't let a MOB mentality squelch her voice or desire to serve.

As the last of the festival committee members hugged each other and filed out of the church, Pastor Donaldson commented, "Well, Rev. Dr., you did it again. You brought calm to a potential storm and moved us toward what is sure to be another successful festival!" She lowered her eyes and beamed. Only ordained ministers were actually "reverends" or could be pastors, but he liked to call Marnie that when he was particularly proud of her. "Your leadership and administrative skills are impressive and steadily improving. I better watch out for my job." *Yeah right. Our church has never had a female pastor in its almost 150-year history.* After doling out a few more perfunctory compliments about other committee members, Pastor Donaldson became more serious. "Please be sure to compile the notes from today's meeting and distribute them to the other pastors in the alliance. Email attachments are fine for most but remember that Pastors Jemmison and Taylor do not believe in the Internet, so please update them via snail mail. In addition, I am a bit concerned about relying on buses from St. Sebastian's. You'd better confirm that. Sometimes our Catholic peers have to wade through a lot of bureaucratic red tape before they can loan out equipment. We don't want to get caught in a bind."

As if reading from an imaginary report, Pastor Donaldson continued to rattle off a laundry list of administrative tasks for Marnie to complete that week. It included: organizing the next ordination meeting; changing the date and time for the youth Bible Trivia Contest; ensuring that everyone was prepared and in place for Sunday's Kickoff Pledge campaign; and confirming all the instructors, including herself, for the four midweek bible study classes. Marnie was aware of most of them; several were new tasks to juggle. Pastor Donaldson was clearly a better delegator than shepherd. She immediately avoided eye contact with him. *At least I have job security.* Ministers were supposed to serve, right? She just wished the other seven ministers at the church served equally.

As their walking debriefing ended, Pastor Donaldson said, "Oh, Marnie, I almost forgot. I have a wonderful opportunity for you. I would like you to develop an eight-part bible study on prayer. Several members have requested an in-depth study on the topic and I agree that the church could really benefit from a strengthened prayer life. You can develop the series as the Holy Spirit leads you and I can review and edit your handouts. Of course, I can be available to help you, but I doubt you'll need me. Exegesis is another one of your strong suits. What can't you do?" His thin lips curved upward and he continued the calm commands. "If possible, I'd love for the series to begin next month and then continue for the two-month period. I'm looking forward to seeing how you will bless this church through your excellent teaching. I can't wait to ordain you, so you can *really* get busy doing the Lord's work." Pastor Donaldson beamed; Marnie's shoulders slumped. *A Shadow Pastor, that's all I am*, Marnie cursed subconsciously.

Shadow Pastor. Marnie created the term, and only used it around close friends, to describe over-worked, under-valued, and under-paid preachers who seemed to perform most of the ministerial work at a church for pastors who largely preached on Sunday morning and served as apostolic window dressing Monday through Saturday. Shadow Pastors tended to have less tenure and fewer letters behind their names, but just as much passion, skill, and expertise as the pastors for whom they worked. Equally important, Shadow Pastors were usually women or a member of some other minority group! *They think we should be glad just to be allowed in the room.* Her brow furrowed.

Later that night, while on a dinner date, Marnie's boyfriend Jeremy diverted the memories of another hectic day. For almost two years, Jeremy attended Bethlehem every other Sunday like clockwork, mainly to support Marnie. He was actually a member of a nearby Presbyterian church. When Marnie teased him about not going to his own church enough, he laughed. "God is everywhere, so I'm sure God won't mind if I attend two churches." She didn't like to admit it, but her heart skipped a bit every time she saw Jeremy enter the doors at Bethlehem. His empathy for her ran deep. He sometimes referred to MOBs, Marnie's "Mean Old Biddies", as "Mean Old Bitches." Sometimes after a particularly harrowing meeting or ambush in the church hallway by some of them, she didn't even correct him. Tonight was no different.

"Marnie, you're the queen of diplomatically disagreeing and deflating unkind remarks," Jeremy said between gulps of sweet tea.

"They must know the inverse relationship between MOBs and millennials. Or am I the only person who realizes this?" she said. "They don't realize that they are chasing away the very people who will sustain the church after they die." Marnie threw up her hands.

"You know how to handle this," he said.

"They think they are the bastions and gatekeepers of all things good, perfect, and holy.

Jeremy, what if those women were once mirror images of me? What if I end up like them, so wedded to my beliefs, values, and traditions that I push away other people who also love God and the Church, but who just think differently about how to do things?"

Jeremy noticed a vein in her temple begin to pulse. "Listen. Don't do that to yourself. You won't end up a MOB. I know it. You know it too. You said some of them mean well. Learn from that. Take the good and throw away the bones," He sighed as her throbbing vein gradually slowed.

As they munched on their Greek salads, Jeremy continued to respond to Marnie's animus and exhaustion. "Most of those old ladies work hard. You've said so yourself. At that age, the church is all many of them have left. Despite the aches, wrinkles, and other ailments that come with time, I think one of the few benefits of growing old is the ability to think you can say anything you want to anybody you want without repercussions. Most folks simply laugh at your candor, ignore you, or attribute your remarks to dementia. Older Christians are particularly guilty of this. It's amazing how God 'tells them' to instruct us, warn us, or reprimand us. Because they are believers, we are more apt to believe them. Bunk!" He chewed on a tomato slice. "Pastor Donaldson just wants to avoid their wrath. That's why he always puts you in charge of those types of events. He knows that, no matter how bad it gets, the people respect and trust you. They know you will do the right thing."

The sides of Marnie's mouth gradually rose. Jeremy was discerning. He, too, came from a long line of churchgoers; he had strong beliefs. However, he often confessed, "Thank God, I am not a minister." Outside of his work as a librarian when they initially met (Marnie admitted that she didn't know male librarians existed), Jeremy was very active in his church's prison ministry. "I try not to get into your church business, but I think your pastor takes advantage of you sometimes. Yeah, we all know you are a genius." He winked. "Come on, what about those jokers on the ministerial staff? From my view, most of them just like to sit in the pulpit Sunday mornings, pray loudly, shout and clap at every opportunity, and suck up to the pastor. None of them work like you do. I can feel your temperature rising, so I'll leave that subject alone for now."

"Let's just enjoy our meal together. I feel like dessert tonight," said Marnie, wanting to both change the subject and eke out a few moments of quite time before getting back to that Bethlehem to-do list.

She jokingly referred to Jeremy as her part-time lover, but he was actually the closest Marnie had ever come to a long-term relationship. That title was also ironic considering that, despite dating for well over two years, they'd never actually had "sex sex." She found his slight paunch, horn-rimmed glasses, and tendency to snort when a joke was particularly funny and sexy. However, Jeremy's patience with her around sex made him even sexier. In truth, she was just as big a nerd as he was.

A strict upbringing that associated pre-marital sex with a certain degree of guilt, fear, and anxiety followed Marnie. That childhood episode when Super Saint had witnessed Minister Peters and Sister White hadn't helped. So much to his dismay, Marnie often quelled passionate moments with

Jeremy by imagining God looking down at them. "No, I won't have God looking at my exposed breasts and your erect penis!" Jeremy's snorting squashed those tense moments. Marnie knew God was omnipotent, omnipresent, and omniscient, but she liked to think that God somehow allowed married couples a bit of privacy during sex that God didn't afford single folks who were breaking the rules.

Although prudish in some sense, subconsciously Marnie also delayed sex with Jeremy because it represented a certain amount of control in a man's world. Barring rape, God forbid, she could decide if and when she wanted to have sex. She liked that, especially when she thought about male-dominated ministerial spaces and continual combat with MOBs. Jeremy was patient, but Marnie wondered how long he would "wait for it" or whether, like her college flame, he would eventually sabotage their relationship by getting a "little bit on the side" from a more willing accomplice. However, for now, spooning on a lazy Saturday morning pleased her almost as much as seeing the top of Jeremy's head rhythmically bobbing between her legs.

Chapter 2:

Oh Little Church of

Bethlehem

Marnie's father had served at Bethlehem before getting his own pastorate outright at St. John's. Now she was an Associate Minister at Bethlehem and, in many ways, continuing his legacy. As a female minister, Marnie was under much more scrutiny from both sides. Some men longed for the "good old days" and desperately clung to biblical interpretations that forbad women from speaking or teaching in church. Additionally, some women either espoused the same beliefs or were envious of Marnie's influential tie to Pastor Donaldson.

Marnie knew that Bethlehem was also full of youth, young couples, new Christians, unchurched visitors and, of course, a smattering of women like Mother Jane. It was for these guileless groups that she continued to work. "I have to be twice as good to get half the respect of the male ministers," she complained aloud. Then she remembered Luke 12:48, to whom much is given, much is required.

Darn scripture that brings solace. However, it was still getting increasingly difficult to squelch her growing resentment at the imbalanced workload among the ministerial staff.

"Every one of you is special and has a unique role here at Bethlehem," Pastor Donaldson had reminded her during their last weekly debriefing. "Marnie, you have many gifts and God wants you to use 'em. Yes, all of the young clergy are in training, but I know I can really depend on you." Yet unlike many of the other pastors for whom she'd worked, Marnie believed that Pastor Donaldson was forthright. She knew that he relied on her because he knew she would always give one hundred and ten percent. Her blood shot eyes cradled by bags attested to that. However, Pastor Donaldson was enabling the other ministers who excelled at being mediocre preachers, teachers, and administrators. And by failing to expose the troubling situation, even Marnie was an enabler. Moreover, the congregations where these ministers would later serve wouldn't get the crucial support they needed and deserved. "You are my right hand man, uh, person. That's why I so look forward to ordaining you soon," Pastor Donaldson had promised. "Now let me know if I assign you too much work. I don't want to do that, but I truly believe that God has a special anointing on you. Eyes have not seen nor ears heard. You know the rest." *Blah, blah, blah*, Marnie had thought. Was Pastor Donaldson stringing her along?

Church politics, low pay, and physical exhaustion aside, Marnie enjoyed being a minister. Although church folks could be challenging and studying the bible often resulted in more questions than answers, she was certain about one thing — ministry was her vocation. She was born to teach, preach, listen, advise, cheer, cajole, confront, and maybe one day, pastor, in a way that only she was destined to do. Marnie's father had said long ago, "If you do what you can, God will show up and do what you can't." Moreover, during those times when Marnie thought she might not be able to read another passage, organize another meeting, consecrate another loaf, teach another class, lead another prayer service, dedicate another squirming infant, calm another conflict, sing another song, or pray over another casket, she somehow did.

"Tell us that story about Jonah and the Whale, David over Goliath, or Daniel in the Lion's Den, Miss Marnie!" eager-faced toddlers begged. "Your sermon last week really helped me get through a rough patch." Another stated, "I never thought about that passage of scripture that way, Minister Hunter. God is good!" God was taking Marnie's sincere efforts and transforming them into something more. Not because of her, but because that's how God works. Yet her bouts between fulfillment and resentment were becoming more frequent. As his "right hand man." Marnie was also responsible for preaching on fifth Sundays or when Pastor Donaldson was on vacation, visiting the sick, and taking Communion to homebound elders.

After her rounds at a local eldercare facility that morning, Marnie maneuvered through traffic looking at her watch to meet Pastor Donaldson. She silently kicked herself for committing, yet again, to be his ecclesiastical wingman. "Let's get on the road. It will take about forty-five minutes to drive to the revival. I'm presiding." He hurried past her toward the driver's side of his Benz. "I rarely travel such distances if I'm not scheduled to preach, but I want to get better acquainted with the new pastor of New Haven Church, Dr. Bradley Jenson. It will also be a good learning experience for you." Marnie would learn more than she anticipated.

Upon entering the sanctuary, Marnie realized their ages of origination were probably the only thing New Haven and Bethlehem had in common. Although the former church was pristine, it was a throwback to traditionalism. New Haven's tracker pipe organ, mammoth cherry chancel, and wall-sized copy of Da Vinci's *Last Supper* contrasted with Bethlehem's instrument section that included a piano, electronic keyboard, and drums as well as its purple and gold ornate banners on which flew the messages "Jesus Saves" and "All Are Welcome." After much debate, Bethlehem's elders and trustees reluctantly agreed to purchase two large screen televisions to display church announcements and song lyrics. "Jumbo-trons won't make the weekly announcements by the church secretary or song books obsolete," Pastor Donaldson assured the cadre of worried seniors. "We can create a spirit-filled worship space where parts of old and new church culture coalesce!" Truth be told, Marnie knew that MOBs would make sure Bethlehem maintained its history. Yet even the most reluctant older members knew that the church needed certain innovations to grow. So fears about the potential death of the church in the current, competitive religious marketplace squelched fears about change. Marnie wondered how New Haven would fare.

The church was already filled with parishioners. Marnie and Pastor Donaldson hurriedly made their way down the left side of the sanctuary toward the pulpit. Neither had ever met Pastor Jenson before, but a nod and extended right hand of an usher sent them in the right direction. During their hearty handshake, Pastor Jenson leaned over and whispered something in Pastor Donaldson's ear. Marnie stretched her neck, but she couldn't hear the exchange. Pastor Donaldson only nodded and returned the smile. He slowly turned and motioned for Marnie to follow him to the pews near the pulpit where the deacons, trustees, and evangelists sat, a sort of ecclesiastical over-flow. She obligingly followed.

Before they could sit, Pastor Jenson hastily intervened and led them both to several empty seats in the pulpit. Pastor Donaldson again nodded and motioned for Marnie to sit next to him. Was that a flash of embarrassment on the host pastor's face? Moreover, why was Marnie the only woman sitting in the pulpit? The church service was festive and transpired without fanfare. During the ride home, Marnie questioned Pastor Donaldson about the earlier fleeting encounter with Rev. Jenson. "Oh, it wasn't anything. He said that he didn't allow women to sit in the pulpit... I guess he changed his mind." She glanced out the window and smiled as the rural scenery rushed by.

Chapter 3:

Train Up a Girl in the Way She

Should Go?

Marnie grew up in the Christian Community faith tradition (often abbreviated "CC"), but at Franklin Interdenominational Seminary, she self-classified as an "independent" student. This decision was more about strategy than denomination because it had given her access to multiple funding sources and inter-denominational internships. She loved the CC history and traditions, but they were notorious for over-working and under-funding seminary students, especially women. It was in such trenches that Shadow Pastors were cultivated. "My finances, my future," abruptly ended one of the few confrontations between Marnie and her father.

An apprentice model was common among pastors who mentored seminary students. Shadow sage clergy. Watch, look, listen, and learn by doing. There were other benefits too. Pastors could get students to do church work without actually paying them. *Pastoral pimps*, Marnie thought after an unusually difficult internship. Some pastors used this training model because they'd gone through it. Still, others believed a busy work schedule reflected students' reasonable service. Marnie earned a Master of Divinity degree in Christian Education and a Doctor of Ministry degree in Pastoral Care and Counseling in four years. Her father, Lee Hunter, helped educate Marnie in terms of both what to do and what *not* to do.

Pastor Lee Hunter

In some ways, the cliché was true — Pastor Lee Hunter was larger than life. In other ways, not so much. Despite eating whatever his heart desired, his svelte five-foot six-inch frame never changed. "You're a darn miracle," his wife once said in gest. His physical stature belied a charismatic personality and presence. Lee Hunter came from a long line of CC pastors. His father, his father's father, and, he'd told; his father's father's father were all pastors in this denomination. Moreover, his earliest predecessors were circuit preachers, pastoring two to three small congregations at a time.

"I remember walking many a country mile as a child to get to the different churches my father pastored," he opined. "Later the distances were even longer when we got that old Chevrolet." Even when he became a minister, tiny country congregations could only afford semi-monthly visits from Pastor Hunter. Yet his young family anticipated delicious Sunday dinners of crispy, golden brown chicken, farm grown vegetables, candied yams gleaming with cinnamon and syrupy brown butter glaze, and homemade yeast rolls.

Congregants, adults and children alike, filled their arms with baskets of sundry foodstuffs, a few dollars from the offering tray, and heaping mounds of love and appreciation. Like his foreparents, somehow the family survived. Lee Hunter could regale listeners for hours. He never romanticized stories. "Marnie, you need to know how harsh some of those times were and how far God has brought our family. You come from a strong line."

Pastor Hunter was also reputed for weaving colorful stories into sermons and bible study lessons. The congregation sat affixed on his every word. He was seminary trained, but Marnie realized that her father's preaching and teaching abilities stemmed from a place of transparency and purity. He didn't have to "add yeast" to a story. His accounts were so vivid that Marnie thought she could actually hear the clicking of the uneven gravel underfoot as he scurried to church and feel the wind rushing through his sandy brown hair as he sat in a quiet, obliging meadow writing a sermon. She could envision paper fans from a local funeral home furiously waving in a tightly packed church and smell the beckoning aroma of fried chicken and peach cobbler. Even when he only spoke above a murmur, Pastor Hunter's words always rang true. Long before Marnie realized or accepted her calling, she had one wish: to be able to command an audience like her father.

In the tradition of many great CC preachers, her father also had a reputation for his attire. Even when that apparel was largely hand-me-downs from his own father, Pastor Hunter always dressed to the nines. After years of scrapping and sacrificing, he could afford suits that were more expensive and treated himself accordingly. However, Marnie's mother, the family accountant, ensured a proper balance between the family's budget and the desires of her fashionista husband. His stylish statements would include Versace, Brooks Brothers, and Armani suits; Prada and Givenchy footwear; silk ties and matching pocket squares; and silver or gold cuff links and tie pins. Yet Pastor Hunter trained Marnie that the external appearance should never overshadow her internal traits or what she was saying. Clothes should draw not distract.

Pastor Hunter would lower his eyes and silently mouth "thank you" when complimented on his attire. Followed by a quick wink at his wife, Shannon Hunter. "Now let's be clear," he acknowledged, "I have difficulty matching black with black, blue with blue, and gray with gray. Your mom is my personal stylist, my publicist, and my everything." Older family and church members told Marnie that her parents had been holding gazes and exchanging fleeting winks for forty years. "You really need to have a doctor check that nervous tick," Marnie chuckled once. Pastor Hunter responded with a wink at Shannon.

Marnie could find little wrong with her dad. However, one thing aggravated her to no end: his lengthy mealtime prayers. Granted altar prayers should be a bit long. You're interceding on behalf of a whole lot of needy people, but during dinner? First, each family member recited a bible verse from memory. Marnie and her gurgling stomach preferred "Jesus wept." Then everyone closed their eyes, held hands, and the praying began. Lee Hunter seemed to consider these prayers the one time the entire family could harness their spiritual powers in one place and for one purpose. So he prayed long and he prayed hard. He took James 5:16 seriously and literally. "Pray one for another, that ye may be healed. The effectual fervent prayer of a righteous man availeth much."

Family, congregants, neighbors, the general public, political leaders, problems like poverty and discrimination, and news events were all included. Moreover, he couldn't leave those birds and ants out of his fervent talk with God! Her mom's soft "Yes", "Amen", and "Hear us, oh God" completed the medley. *Enough already. Can I just eat my chicken?* However, Marnie dared not interrupt their family ritual. After enough hand squeezes by their mother, she and her siblings learned to control their fidgeting and anticipation. They would still cautiously open one eye and search of silent signs of support from each other. Pastor Hunter usually prayed so long that the food got cold. Cold chicken could be stomached, but cold *oatmeal!* Like Super Saint, Mrs. Hunter eventually saved the day by ferreting away enough money to purchase a microwave.

After his eventual "Amen" came the tinging of forks on plates, bowls clinking, and growing chatter. "How was school today? Didn't you have an exam today? What do you think about so and so on last night's news?" Meals were a time to feed the family's bodies and spirits. When she became a teenager, Marnie realized that their family meals were about fellowship, bonding, conversation, queries, and debates. They were periods when Lee and Shannon Hunter taught their children to question, mull, self-reflect, and ultimately, think critically. It was also during those times that Pastor Hunter modeled the importance of praying to God and one way to do it. Even now, their family's Sunday dinners would seem strangely empty without her father's prayers.

Yet Marnie knew well the dangers of holding people in high esteem. "Even well-meaning people have feet of clay," Lee Hunter warned. "I'm not trying to dissuade you from having faith in people. Just be cautious about putting them on pedestals, myself included. Frailty thy name is humanity," he paraphrased. "Anyway, people's beauty doesn't lie in unattainable perfection, but in how they work every day to lead good lives and do their best despite imperfections. All have sinned and fallen short." Marnie couldn't help but place her father on a tiny pedestal. "I've seen a lot, but my mantra hasn't changed. 'Believe in God, the good in people, and the good in yourself, scars and all.'" Would Pastor Hunter feel the same way if he knew the truth about Marnie's scars?

Chapter 4:

Is There a Mentor in the

House?

Two preachers, two teachers, and a hooker walk into a bar — sounds like the making of a crude joke. Yet this motley crew of characters represent the five individuals who had an indelible influence on Marnie's life and vocation. She fondly referred to them as the Fabulous Five!

Mrs. Desdemona Stevenson

Mrs. Desdemona Stevenson was a handful as much as her name was a mouthful. One particularly tense day in class, Marnie seemed to trip over every word of a carefully planned speech. Mrs. Stevenson looked her keenly in the eyes and calmly but firmly commanded, "Marnie, you won't get anywhere trying to be like everyone else. You aren't like everyone else. You must give yourself permission to be excellent." The young girl's mouth fell open. *But I'm only in the sixth grade!* Marnie thought.

The cherub-faced teacher seemed to read her mind and retorted, "I don't care what grade you're in. I need excellence!" She placed her hands on her hips as if posing then flung her long red ascot over her shoulder. "Anything less is a waste of my time and yours. You must always do your very best. I demand it." Further clarifying the chain of command, she continued, "God demands it!"

How did Mrs. Stevenson know the great lengths Marnie went to: attempting to chatter on about boys, frilly frocks, lip-gloss, and the latest Osmond Brothers' lyrics or lying that algebra was *so hard*? Had this teacher realized that Marnie would much rather be running through grass or that she couldn't care less about flyaway strands of her hair and smudges on her jumper? Had she known how the inquisitive young girl actually adored all of her classes and voraciously read every book within reach? Mrs. Stevenson was a mind reader, so she had to know about Marnie's dreams of becoming a writer and having her own radio show. Marnie desperately wanted to fit in, but it was futile. Despite the passage of time and words of wisdom others shared since, Marnie always remembered those words. *Give yourself permission to be excellent.* Both a challenge and a command, they became Marnie's own mantra that she graciously shared with anyone needing to be similarly inspired. No one could replace the irrepressible Desdemona Stevenson. Almost two decades later, Rev. Dr. Irene Calgary continued where Mrs. Stevenson left off.

Dr. Irene Calgary

Marnie met Dr. Calgary on her first day at Franklin Seminary. Dressed in a pale yellow argyle sweater set, khaki skirt, pearls, and sensible shoes, she stood in stark contrast to most female clergy Marnie knew. "Wow! You're an ordained minister? You're the first one I've met in our denomination. You're like a unicorn." Marnie almost shook her right hand off. She was used to female ministers donned in sky blue and sage green suits and matching red bottoms, or the other extreme, staid, androgynous figures wearing so much starched white that they resembled nuns. No matter the attire, they all dangled lap scarves and challenged young women to lower their hemlines and voices. But not Dr. Calgary! Marnie included her among the biblical bastions such as Dorcas, Esther, Candace, and Priscilla. Yet these women were often relegated to second-class citizenship in religious spaces. Tradition dictated it. Even in Marnie's present, they primarily led traditionally gendered programs such as Sunday school and administration.

"When I was a child," Dr. Calgary said, "I questioned my father. Why do only men preachers get to sit in the pulpit and women preachers sit on the first pew next to the deacons? Why aren't there any women deacons?" Her eyes narrowed. "I promised, 'When I get grown, I will never attend a church like that!'" She stomped her foot. *Super Saint found a kindred spirit!* "Students, we're fighting an uphill battle. Many church men espouse those kinds of traditions. Truth be told, many women like them do too, but things are changing. We all have to fight the good fight." She provided a litany of women who continued to preach and teach about God's unconditional love, Jesus' sacrificial nature, the transforming power of the Holy

Spirit, and the reconciliatory work of the Church. For Marnie, Dr. Calgary was living proof of how women ministers, and their male allies, slowly but surely chipped away at the most insidious features of church patriarchy.

"Some people might mistake Dr. Calgary for a grandmother and ask her favorite cookie recipe, but don't get it twisted." Marnie gushed praised to her parents after a lively class with the senior scholar and community activist.

"I love children — other people's children." Dr. Calgary threw her head back and cackled. "Cooking? Hate it. However, I welcome any tasty treats you want to cook for me." The warmth of her widening eyes enveloped the class, but the levity was short-lived. "My life's mission is to spiritually gird up each of you. Whether you like it or not," she spoke above a whisper, but with certainty and authority.

Dr. Calgary was a world-renowned preacher and teacher whose forte in Christian education, church administration, and youth ministry made her a stronghold at the seminary. She was also a formidable model for anyone who questioned a woman's ability to lead. The cleric decreed her mantra at the start of every class. "As God's elect, clergy are called to transform the world! If *you* as seminarians ever hope to accomplish this Herculean feat, you must partner with *me* to ferret out any and all foibles and flaws that could slow your race." She continued, "I don't expect you to be perfect. God knows I'm not. I do expect you to be cognizant of your imperfections, able to harness them, and become humbled during the process." For Dr. Calgary, hearing a person's story was the key to understanding them, helping them better understand themselves, and cultivating their unique voice. She then looked intently at the terrified faces in the room and said, "Now tell me your story."

Marnie swore that Dr. Calgary and her father were long-lost siblings because both were masterful storytellers. Somehow, this teacher's ability surpassed that of her father, although Marnie would die before admitting it to her dad. As a female minister, Dr. Calgary understood what it meant to be different from her peers and was often misunderstood because of it. No matter how thoughtful and empathetic, Marnie's father could never walk in those shoes. He could never fully understand male privilege, sexism, gendered stereotypes, or the everyday life of female clergy in a predominately-male religious world. Dr. Calgary understood! Moreover, she helped Marnie and other female ministers find the words to articulate both their common experiences and unique challenges.

"It is a must that you become more discerning of people and principalities that perpetuate prejudices against women. Try saying that five times fast." Her eyes danced even when discussing difficult topics. Somehow, Dr. Calgary waged a frontal attack against gender inequality without: man-hating; making women feel superior; rejecting men with good intentions, but minimal follow through; or falling into the common "us versus them" trap that made progress toward equality so sluggish.

"Men in the house," she called one day, "You are needed in this fight. You are crucial allies in the war for inclusivity and equality for all God's children."

Through storytelling, case studies, biblical critique, and class discussions, Dr. Calgary taught wide-eyed students: to build bridges across differences; activist strategies; ways to equip people to know better and, by extension, do better; and, to challenge the status quo. "Men in the house," she continued, "You must also know that by championing equality, you will surely be targets for shame and isolation by male peers who like things just the way they are. So ministers, male and female, get ready to rumble!"

The teacher also shared her story of how God strengthened her voice. "With a rapidly expanding belly, my husband and I decided to take one final vacation to the Catskills. We also realized that the arrival of our first child would mean many months, possibly years, without the time, energy, or money to travel again. A small battalion of family members accompanied us. I imagined hiking along picturesque preserve trails, sipping hot cocoa in front of a roaring fire, and watching family members ski down Hobbs Mountain. These would be great memories to share with our child." She breathed in deeply as if harnessing sufficient air to continue.

"A freak snowstorm buffeted the tiny plane. The wings and windshield frosted over, requiring an emergency landing. Save me and my husband, everyone on board, including our unborn child, perished in the crash," Dr. Calgary uttered. "I lost both my will to live and my voice. I sat mute and transfixed in bed for much of the year; it took that long for my body to heal. It would take much longer for me to become whole. My husband, Jim, God bless his soul, swallowed his own grief to nurse me back to health. I would need him all the more when I learned that, as a result of the accident, I could no longer conceive children."

"How did you make it?" an impatient student interrupted, as her classmates shot darts with their eyes in her direction.

Dr. Calgary seemed to be in a daze. "Like I did after the crash, I crawled on my belly through a dark, tight night with only a sliver of light as a guide. God was there with me. I knew it. I pulled my body along and grew stronger with each press. All the while, I used my imagination to travel to distant places as I slowly, but surely, moved toward the exit from the pain. Something miraculous happened as I drew closer to my goal and a new beginning that always exists when we take such a journey." The class drew in a collective breath. "My tears are now tears of joy because I know, first hand, the healing power of God's love as well as how that same love can manifest across time and space in family members and friends." Dr. Calgary's voice became strong, but tempered by the realities, both positive and negative, of life and the wisdom that ensues for people willing to accept them.

"My story continues to unfold beyond my wildest imagination." Her voice popped with excitement and wonder. "Now I'm blessed to parent thousands of students over decades as a professor! Wonderful students like each of you!" Dr. Calgary's book on healing and acceptance entitled *Finding My Voice Again* spent twenty-six weeks on the nonfiction bestseller list; she donated all proceeds to programs to help people who experience the loss of loved ones. Moreover, she refused to accept any of the lucrative offers from large seminaries that constantly sought her but remained committed to Franklin. Under her tutelage, Marnie honed her speaking, writing, and teaching skills and found her own voice. Like her beloved mentor, Marnie wanted to become unapologetically true to every dimension of her life and all its possibilities — scars and all. However, the young cleric's journey seemed somehow derailed. Maybe some scars   can't   heal.

Chapter 5: Pastors, Preachers, and Pimps

Full seminary funding required Marnie to serve as a clergy intern at a local church. With little control over the assignment, she experienced some unpleasant matches. First, there was Pastor Lyndon Pond known for his predilection of unceremoniously embracing female interns, followed by Bishop Terrance Shane whose fire and brimstone sermons on Sunday were only matched by his screeching commands at the ministerial trainees on Monday. However, Marnie's most troubling experience occurred her third year in seminary at Friendship House under the pastorate of Rev. Chester Cargill. *What a godsend*, Marnie thought! The internship would pay her living expenses and incidentals. She was sadly mistaken.

Pastor Chester Cargill

Marnie should've been suspicious that Friendship House needed an intern despite already having five ministers. Why did Pastor Cargill scan her résumé and hire her on the spot? The denomination had recruited him to turn the church around. His spiritual gifts were many: preaching, singing, and teaching. However, like an abandoned puppy, he seemed to be searching for friends. Marnie knew that a pastor's congregants don't usually make good confidants. Unfortunately, nobody told Pastor Cargill.

"Please, please, call me Pastor Chet. Everybody does. We're all family here," he chortled. "Oh, daughter of Eve, welcome to Friendship House, the place of solace and safety for God's elect." He sounded like he was trying to sell her a used Dodge minivan. "No matter what you hear, Friendship House is just that. We have some detractors out there. Haters got to hate, but we just show them love. Love erases a multitude of sins!" His arms flailed and his hands landed squarely on Marnie's. *Yuck*, she thought, *he gives the phrase "lean in" a completely new meaning.* So went their encounters. His incessant compliments and innuendos ("you're *really* looking good today, Minister Hunter" or comments about sexual tensions among the ranks) made bile rise in her throat. Marnie looked passed them, especially every time she deposited a paycheck. Over time, the prattling about his problems exhausted Marnie. All the while, the church pews were chronically empty and a new member wasn't in sight. Friend House performed more funerals than baby dedications, a Seminary 101 rule that this church was in trouble. Sometimes, Marnie wanted to shriek, "Shut the hell up!"

One of Marnie's spiritual gifts was administration that included organizing, prioritizing, leading, and translating broader visions into reality. "Marnie, I would love for you to become our church administrator." His voice lingered a bit too long on the verb. Her initial elation was short lived. Pastor Chet explained her role to the other ministers and members, but few seemed ready for change. Younger couples were supportive, but the other ministers struggled with the new process. The MOB was on the prowl. The dozen or so male members were from families with long histories at that church. They knew the score and either quietly acquiesced to the MOB or swiftly exited after the benediction not to be seen again until the following Sunday.

One month into her internship, three older women who learned that Pastor Chet asked her to organize the newly instituted Women's Week cornered Marnie in the back hall of the church. "We appreciate your zeal, Ms. Marnie, but clearly you are new here and there are things you just don't know," said the woman with the biggest hat and biggest mouth. "You just don't know *our* ways or traditions. Things must be done decently and in order." The other women's heads bobbled vigorously in support.

"The plans I presented were already approved by the church board," Marnie said. Why hadn't Pastor Chet attended the kick-off meeting to address such concerns? He was always suspiciously absent when there was either work to do or conflict to resolve. Energized for work, the MOB ate conflict for breakfast!

"We don't care who approved *your* program. The *women* of Friendship House didn't! We won't have programs and activities forced upon us! Exactly how old are you anyway? What is your denomination?" Another woman snapped through pinched lips. A male minister chanced upon the scene, grinned sheepishly, and promptly disappeared down the hall.

"Sisters, Pastor Chet asked me to present several events, discuss them, and get feedback and next steps from the women of the church. That's what I did. You are correct, I am new here, but I'm here to help. That's all I'm trying to do — help." After a pregnant pause, the three women shirked and stomped away. The thirty-second encounter left Marnie spent. *What gall.* Nothing was resolved for that MOB, but everything was clear to her. Marnie headed straight for the pastor's office.

"So sorry that you experienced that, Minister Hunter," Pastor Chet lobbed a veiled reprimand. "Had I known you couldn't handle the ladies, I would have attended the meeting."

"It's not about whether I can handle them, Pastor, it's about a church culture that allows such disrespect for members in general and ministers in particular. I have never been spoken to like that in my entire life, let alone in a church. I don't plan to be spoken to that way again." Her forehead furrowed.

"Calm down." she saw him catch himself before rolling his eyes, "They just need to get to know you. I promise. Things will get better." They didn't.

Over the next few months, Marnie realized that it was common for the revolving door of members to disrespect the pastor, other ministers, and each other. It even affected its youngest members. Despite lengthy rehearsals on Saturdays, on Sundays, the children's choir would routinely stand stone-faced with their tiny mouths shut like traps and their tiny hands folded either resolutely across their tiny chests or on their tiny hips. Pastor Chet handled the problems by ignoring them and spending as little time as possible at the church. "Office hours? That's what cell phones are for," he retorted. Marnie or a female evangelist usually taught midweek bible study. Their male peers showed up periodically, typically to gobble up the snacks or if they heard that Pastor Chet might be there, and scowled during the entire teaching/learning hour. On Sundays, they would arrive early to jockey for a seat in the pulpit closest to Pastor Chet.

Over the course of a semester, Marnie developed and taught multiple bible study sessions, re-organized the church's administrative processes, and led the new ministers' monthly training. Marnie hoped she was making some difference. More and more members said that they enjoyed her preaching, teaching, and leadership. Yet she believed that for many of them, church attendance was a ritual akin to weekly team bowling, watching their favorite television show, or a beauty shop appointment. The MOB held Friendship House by its spiritual throat and continued to make Marnie's life a living hell. She refused to accept or condone the disrespect increasingly lobbed in her direction.

"You better get used to it," nonchalantly replied one of the older women that Marnie considered a friend. "Being a Christian means enduring long-suffering. No matter how folks act at Friendship House, you *have* to love 'em."

Marnie retorted, "Ma'am, you were born and raised in this church. It's all you know. I can assure you, Friendship House is not the norm. It does not have to be this way." She felt heat rising on the back of her neck. "Don't you wonder why we rarely get new members? Or why our Sunday school and bible study numbers are dropping? Why should I get used to that?" The elderly woman looked away.

Marnie came to a stark conclusion. Rev. Chet wasn't a pastor; he was a preacher. Despite exegetical prowess, his sermons strategically avoided topics like inequality. Friendship House sponsored one of the largest feeding programs in the city, but Rev. Chet never challenged members to work to help reduce poverty. Like too many churches, Marnie thought, it continued to address symptoms of social problems and not their roots. Marnie faced the undeniable truth that Pastor Chet couldn't shepherd if his life depended on it! He feigned affection and interest, but only responded to his favorite members or upon MOB threat. Marnie's best friend, Monica, responded to her grievances. "Like so many pastors, that Rev. Chet is crazy — crazy like a fox. He knows that to reach his ministerial goals of pastoring a big church and having big coffers, he will need a *harem* of Holy Spirit-filled women to do the heavy lifting. That means you." *A Shadow Pastor*, Marnie winced. "Get with the program, girl." Marnie was idealistic and inexperienced back then, now she knew better. Yet could she stave off pessimism to follow her calling?

During that internship, Marnie realized the importance of discernment, self-love, and self-care. No more ignoring sexism, no matter the cost. She now understood the difference between the "work of the church" and "church work" and vowed to pursue the former and avoid the latter. Marnie experienced another epiphany. She imagined what female ministers could actually accomplish if they focused on their own vocations. Didn't God give them dreams and abilities? Did they question themselves? Did they decide that someone else's dreams were more important or achievable? On the other hand, maybe colic, cooking, playdates, organizing schedules, and day jobs simply sapped their dreams. Maybe female ministers, like so many other women, were just plain tired. Was vicariously experiencing success through their pastors easier? Maybe some success was better than nothing.

At the end of her stint, Pastor Chet chimed, "Minister Marnie, has it been six months already! Time flies when you're having fun." *Have we been in the same universe?* He continued before she could actually respond. "You must stay on with us. You must!" He offered a hefty salary and her own office. Marnie admitted that her work resulted in some positive outcomes. Administrative processes now worked like a well-oiled machine, bible study numbers were up, and Women's Week was a success. She was even a welcomed preaching alternative to the pastor. "Your presence has renewed me, Minister Marnie," Pastor Chet heaped praise. Marnie shouldered slumped and her mouth drooped. Minister Marnie Hunter decided then and there — *I will no longer be the Shadow Pastor for the venerable Pastor Chester Cargill or for anyone else!*

Rev. Benjamin B. James

The Friendship House fiasco was behind Marnie, but still wreaked havoc on her psyche. She was about to graduate from seminary and eager to find a church. No church was perfect, but Marnie was searching for a place where people were so busy doing the work of the church that they just didn't have the time or interest for drama. She needed a *church home*. Her internships required a lot of church hopping. Now Marnie yearned for spiritual and non-spiritual support, sanctuary, and stability. Most importantly, she wanted to make her own choice. That prospect sent a ripple of excitement down her spine; she could hear Sinatra crooning, *I did it my way*. One Sunday, Clark Street megachurch beckoned her. Its campus swallowed several city blocks, yet Marnie had driven by it for years. There she met Rev. Benjamin B. James and things were never quite the same.

Marnie had nothing against large churches, nor was she attracted to them either. Something about the bravado of certain megachurch televangelists did make her blood rise. *Why the extravagant lifestyles, stadium-sized churches, and emphasis on sowing seeds for personal wealth?* Moreover, she felt no sympathy for the two larger than life pastors recently indicted for tax evasion. She was livid at any pastor who fed the hungry masses weekly doses of candy-coated, pie-in-the-sky theology that blamed the poor and sick for their predicaments.

She saw the ravages of poverty, lack of healthcare, and neglect up-close during her summer missionary work in Appalachia and inner city Detroit where God-fearing, hard-working people struggled to make ends meet. She would rail to Monica, "These folks love God, country, and family. They've done nothing to deserve their fate except be born into a world that places the value of a dollar above the worth of people. Don't roll your eyes at me. This is not about being a tree hugger. It's more than that and you know it! Society is a respecter of persons, especially if you have big bucks!" So, armed with a healthy dose of ambivalence, Marnie entered Clark Street's stained-glass doors.

The sanctuary held at least three thousand people but felt surprisingly intimate due to the cadre of affable ushers strategically stationed to greet you. A wash of friendly faces, handshakes, and hugs from people on and around her immediate pew welcomed Marnie. *Interesting.* A praise team sang initially, but a choir also rendered a spiritual, a hymn, and a gospel song. *Mhhmm, a liturgy,* she made another mental note. Drums, a small string section, and an amazing saxophone player accompanied a pipe organ and piano. Marnie appreciated the combination of traditional and contemporary worship elements. Another mental note. *How have I missed this church all these years?* She swayed to the new wave rendition of "What a Friend We Have in Jesus?" *One of my favorite hymns, but with a twist.* Her mental note bin was stuffed. Pastor James' sermon was icing on the cake. She joined that Sunday.

Marnie attended the requisite ten-week New Members course that was team-taught by a woman and a man the following week. Pastor James popped in every class. "Just checking in on my new members," he would say. "Got any questions? Concerns? No question is inappropriate. Or you can call or text me." His eyes beamed as he shook every hand. His brief presence didn't overshadow the instructors' authority but gave Marnie the impression that he wanted to get to know *his* new members.

Clark Street was definitely a large church with a small church feel. Marnie realized the difference between a megachurch televangelist and Rev. James, a local pastor who cultivated a large church over time.

The former strategically used social media to reach virtual members. Local, national, or even international community outreach programs were usually uncommon. To be fair, she knew several local megachurches that sponsored impressive feeding programs and international missions, yet most seemed content spreading the Gospel over the airwaves without spreading their considerable resources to the needy.

Not Clark Street. It did televise and stream programs, but the church tethered the local community. Marnie rattled off the list to Monica. "We've got low-cost housing, an elder care center and hospice facility, an accredited school for PreK to the twelfth grade, a mobile clinic, a grocery store, and extensive substance abuse and HIV/AIDS programs. Oh, did I mention, not one, not two, but three daycare centers. All the ministries are organized through community development corporations. "

"Yeah, yeah, Clark Street is the bomb." Monica beamed.

Marnie continued. "They are called cafeteria-styled programs because…"

"Yeah. Yeah. I know, Marnie. I'm a minister too, remember," her friend said.

"The church is literally open twenty-four hours a day, seven days a week to meet the religious and non-religious needs of members and community." Marnie finally caught her breath. "People respond by joining, volunteering, and paying tithes and offerings." She knew that Clark Street wasn't a utopia. Yet something exciting was happening there that drew the young cleric. After Pastor James confirmed that she completed seminary, Marnie became a ministerial trainee.

Given a ministerial staff of well over twenty-five people, Marnie didn't expect to do much *real* work at Clark Street, only perfunctory introductions of outside speakers or substitute bible class teacher. *Newbies gotta pay their dues,* she thought. She was wrong. "We are so blessed to have four ministerial trainees." Pastor James' lips curled upward. "I pray that we will all become friends. I've assigned each of you a prayer partner from the group and we will all met weekly. Every minister here at Clark Street has a specific role to play in the life of the church based on your spiritual gifts and the congregational needs. Each of you will be crucial to our ministry." His eyes and smile widened further. "You've met the Associate Pastor, Rev. Regina Chiefs; she's my right-hand person." Marnie liked his inclusive language. "You can always reach me. I am here for you!" *Was this a stump speech?* Marnie wondered.

"Each of you have been educated, equipped, and empowered for ministry." *More buzz words?* Her brow wrinkled. He proved her wrong again. Unlike crazy Chet Cargill, he took great pains to shepherd his flock. "Marnie, you've been as quiet as a church mouse," he remarked privately at the close of one session. "I want you to serve based on your personality. I also want to encourage you to be confident about your gifts. Be your best self at all times. I have complete confidence in you." *Give myself permission to be excellent.* Pastor James channeled Desdemona Stevenson. Moreover, he motivated female trainees as insistently as male ones. Over time, they became a surrogate family as they all worked together at the church and in the community.

Marnie had a slight crush on her mentor. His wife, Chase, was a combination of Mother Teresa, Eleanor Roosevelt, and Mary McLeod Bethune, trapped in the body of a supermodel. That green-eyed monster would've reared its ugly head, but Chase was so kind. Marnie forgave Pastor James that one flaw, embracing a conventional model of female beauty. He was so upstanding on all other accounts. *No harm in daydreaming*, she thought. Marnie remembered a one-dime store fantasy when Pastor James' limber arms, nimble fingers, and warm mouth searched the deep recesses of her body. She woke to find her right hand deep within the recesses of her panties and her cat, China Doll, licking her face.

Monica howled when Marnie shared that story. "You're in a pre-mance. Get it, preachers combined with romance — pre-mance. Or maybe it's a min-mance...ministers and romance. You get it!" Monica almost dropped her wine glass. Marnie's cheeks turned crimson. "Aw, come on." Monica rubbed her friend's shoulder. "There's no shame here. Fantasies are a normal sign that you are, well, normal."

Pastor James knew exactly what each of the ministerial trainees needed developmentally to become pastors, teachers, counselors, musicians, and all-around leaders. "Yes, we are called to feed the flock spirituality. We are also called to combat racism, classism, poverty, and other social problems no matter where they are found," he charged the trainees. Yet Pastor James was sensitive to the unique challenges female ministers faced. "Each of you must find your own voice. I can help, but this is your own journey. God chose you for ministry based on your unique personalities, gifts, and skills. Female ministers, you don't have to preach like men, look like men, and act like us." He slowly eyed each of them. Marnie always pushed back against the pressure to conform; pushing back was so much easier at Clark Street. "Corporate conformity didn't come from God. It was man-made. So it belongs in a corporation, not in a congregation." *Amen*, thought Marnie.

Under Pastor James' tutelage, Marnie was able to apply everything she learned in seminary. She preached. She taught. She led. Moreover, she laughed and learned! She also received hands-on practice performing funerals, weddings, baby dedications, and baptisms — all the activities ministers needed to excel. She learned firsthand that the buoyancy of the water in the baptismal pool enabled her to immerse a fidgeting man twice her size. "We do better, when we know better," Pastor James always said. Marnie wanted to do and know everything! Yet the more she learned, the more questions emerged about theology, the nature of sin, seemingly contradictory scriptures, and work-life balance. Most importantly, she wondered whether her past sins that fateful night when she received her scars made her unworthy to follow her calling.

Desi, Doritos, and Doing Ministry

Marnie met the fifth and final member of the Fab Five during Vacation Bible School when the woman stumbled into Clark Street church. As she sat devouring a bag of nacho-flavored Doritos between tear-filled hysterics, Desi said, "I'm trying to get away from my boyfriend. He beats me. I need help," she pleaded between chomps. Although it was only about fifty degrees, she wore a pair of soiled khaki cargo shorts, a faded black tank top, no bra, and worn flip-flops. Her knobby, ashen knees matched her skeletal shoulders, arms, and hands. Desi fought in vain to control her involuntarily twitching frame. Marnie saw lint in her matted hair and sleep in her bloodshot eyes. Both Marnie and the other minister on duty, Reese Collins, noticed the shadow of a week-old black eye. Scratches peppered Desi's neck, face, and arms. She couldn't have been older than twenty-three, she looked twice that.

"I… I need to get into a drug rehab place. I got… to get my crap together. Can somebody help me get a bed somewhere? I need a ride home to get some clothes too. You got anymore Doritos?" Marnie tried in vain to call Pastor James, Rev. Chiefs, and several other ministers. *Darn, straight to voicemail.* Marnie felt an ache of uncertainty in her gut and her hands sweating. Although several years her senior, Reese peered at Marnie as if to say, what should we do? *I wonder if this is how withdrawals feel?* Was Desi's life in danger? What would happen to this poor soul if they didn't help her?

The two ministers made an executive decision to intervene. After a few phone calls, they got Desi a bed in a drug rehab center downtown. However, her check-in was 3:00 p.m. that day or she'd lose her slot. Marnie called Pastor James again. *Shoot, where is he?* Marnie tried to convince herself, *this is ministry on the ground — in the real world!* "Calm down, Desi. We got you a spot in rehab."

"Oh, God! Thank you! Thank you!" Desi cried while still hugging the bag of Doritos. Marnie exhaled as she and Reese exchanged accomplished looks. They were doing what Christ commanded. They watched as the frail woman devoured a children's VBS lunch, including several batches of chicken nuggets and sugar cookies, between gulps of chocolate milk. "Come on, Desi. We've got to get you to that center on time," said Marnie.

Marnie's eyed widened as they drove to Desi's apartment in a sketchy part of the city. Marnie and Reese eyed each other nervously, but nodded — sometimes God's work might involve danger. Marnie thought, what if Shadrach, Meshach, and Abednego gave in to pressure from the King? What if Daniel saw the lion's den and folded? What kind of world would it now be if Jesus Christ bolted from the cross? Desi interrupted her thoughts, "Would you come in and help me pack? We need to be in and out before Joe gets here!" Tiny beads of sweat pooled on Marnie's forehead.

They tiptoed into the disheveled studio apartment. Marnie forced the vomit back at the putrid smell that attacked them at the door. Marnie saw some shocking scenes during her mission trips, but nothing prepared her for that day in her own backyard. Clothing, dirty dishes, empty beer cans, broken wine bottles, and drug paraphernalia littered the one-roomed unit. A plaid, sunken sofa lay against one wall and a stained mattress lay on the floor opposite it. More dirty dishes also cluttered a small kitchen sink and two-burner stove top. A faded floral sheet extending to the ceiling on a jute rope provided makeshift privacy for the commode. Roaches, both dead and scampering, were in eyeshot and several popped rattraps lay unattended near the couch. Marnie didn't see a shower or refrigerator. It was a hovel in the richest nation in the world. "Hurry!" Desi barked. "I said I don't know when he's coming back!"

The three women crammed mounds of clothes, clean and not, into large garbage bags. It wasn't lost on Marnie that they could stuff all of Desi's worldly possessions in plastic bags used to discard trash. They exited the apartment, peeking around every corner, expecting to see Desi's boyfriend. Marnie didn't remember breathing until the apartment building was in her rearview mirror. A few hours later, Marnie and Reese signed; Desi was checked in at the center and taking her first steps toward recovery. Marnie was asleep before her head hit the pillow that night. Exhausted, but accomplished. She confronted the real world and beat it back!

The next morning, Marnie learned that an emergency had detained Pastor James and the other ministers the prior day. However, he was in his office early waiting for Marnie and Reese. *He wants to congratulate us for a job well done!* The pastor stared across his desk at each of them for what seemed like an eternity before speaking. "Ministers Hunter and Collins, I take it you were quite busy yesterday." Because he referred to them formally, Marnie knew that praise wouldn't be forthcoming. Her toothy grin disappeared and the office seemed suddenly claustrophobic. "Although I commend your initiative in trying to help Desi Luther yesterday, I want to express my great, great concern about your decisions." *How did he know Desi's last name?* Marnie wondered. Clearly, someone updated Pastor James about the situation.

"Yes, you showed great unconditional love, kindness, and support for a desperate soul in need.

I applaud you," he continued. "However, your actions put yourselves in possible danger and made the church potentially liable in several ways." Marnie's heart sank as he provided details about which the two-naïve trainees were unaware. "Yes, you did help Desi get into drug rehab. That would have been praise-worthy — had she stayed. Unfortunately, the attendant found her bed empty when they checked on her this morning. Her whereabouts are unknown." Marnie and Reese stared at each other. Marnie's shoulders sagged. "Desi is a well-known prostitute in this area. Clark Street has helped her from time to time over the years with food and small expenses," said Pastor James. "I reached out to Desi myself many times to encourage her to get help for her crack addiction. She declined each time." He paused and licked his lips. "Joe is her pimp."

Feeling duped, Marnie's left foot tapped uncontrollably as she thought about the possible danger they escaped. Scripture was true; God looks after babes and fools. She and Reese were a little bit of both. Pastor James then explained how they should've handled the situation without putting anyone in harm's way. He described the church ministries to contact, scriptures to provide, questions to gauge the seriousness of a situation, and other local agencies. Marnie appreciated how Pastor James turned a reprimand into a teaching moment without shaming them or belittling Desi.

A few months later, Marnie saw Desi on a corner near Clark Street. "I got rid of Joe. I work for myself now. Thanks for what you did. I guess I'm not ready for rehab. Pray for me."

"I will." Marnie kept that promise.

"What's that bible verse you mentioned when I saw you last time?" said Desi.

"Romans 8:31. What shall we say to these things? If God is for us, who can be against us?" Marnie replied.

"Yeah, I like that," said Desi.

Because Desi wouldn't take handouts, now every two weeks, Marnie bought her a twenty-dollar bag of Doritos and they laughed and talked for an hour.

Thanks to seventy-five dollars and online ordinations, today you could throw a rock and hit a minister. Much more was required of God's elect. In countless ways, the Fabulous Five taught Marnie that truth. Marnie swore off being used by pastors again. Moreover, she now picked the meat and threw away the bones when confronting a challenge. Yet each time she rubbed the deep, ebony scars etching the back of her arms, Marnie wondered, would that be enough?

Chapter 6:

Working Hard and Hard at

Working — The Seminary

Sisters

Marnie looked forward to the monthly get-togethers with her three best friends. They called each other the Seminary Sisters. Although Marnie was initially skeptical about whether they could keep it up, the Seminary Sisters had been meeting like clockwork since graduation. What started as a book club to encourage them to read something other than the bible devolved into a free for all. Sometimes it was dinner and a movie or a day trip to an estate sale, but usually the group ended up sitting around one of their living rooms talking shop until, several bottles of Rees-lings later, they felt renewed.

Each woman held impressive post-seminary ministerial positions: Monica pastored a multicultural church; Siobhan was the minister of music at a suburban megachurch; and Percy was a senior administrator in her denomination. After five years, their monthly gatherings inevitably turned into rap sessions about their lives, loves, and ministries.

"I'm so glad to see you guys," Marnie called over her shoulder as she hastily filled four glasses with chardonnay. "Don't get me wrong, I know how blessed we all are. We have unbelievable opportunities to follow God's path for our lives."

Siobhan cut in. "But we need to be able to let our hair down." She swirled her neck from side to side. Their relationships were forged in the fire of Old and New Testament classes, sermon rehearsals, celebrations, dating trials, family traumas, and, of course, preparation for Marnie's impending ordination. Marnie credited the three women with maintaining her sanity. Marnie knew that curiosity was getting the best of them, but she had yet to share the story behind the scars on her elbows and arms. At least Marnie felt safe wearing short-sleeved shirts around them.

Marnie loved Siobhan's quirky candor. She was much more spirited than Marnie could ever be. An expert at both the piano and organ, she possessed perfect pitch and a four octave-range voice. When she sang and played, that cascade of crimson hair bounced in time. Even her freckles danced! Once after too many empty wine bottles lay around the room, Marnie said, "Siobhan, you're so... so... striking. You sure you aren't mixed with something?"

Her friend winked. She drawled, "Yes, dawwlling," leaning back to expose the expanse of her neck, "I'm mixed with everything!" Siobhan's physical beauty was undeniable. Most women could easily hate her if she wasn't so unassuming. When they met in Preaching 101, Marnie loved the bohemian ingénue instantly. Marnie was traditional. Siobhan, not so much. However, they never judged each other; neither was too liberal nor conservative for the other.

Siobhan had been immediately snatched up by Cornerstone Church and married its pastor soon after. "I know this marriage will last," she had shared during their girl's night out right before her wedding day. "We're both committed to ministry and sexually... inquisitive." Marnie blushed every time she saw Siobhan's stolid mate and thought about their secret. Siobhan was actually the most charismatic preacher among them. However, she decided to focus on music and "leave the preaching to dear hubby." Marnie believed she didn't want to compete with her mate directly or indirectly. As co-pastor, Siobhan influenced the church's direction without upsetting tradition.

"You won't believe my week at church," cried Siobhan, well into her third glass of wine. "We are preparing for our annual Spring Cantata and folks are already vying for solos. Even that Mary Ladler, who couldn't hold a tune if it had a handle... I don't think so!" She took another quick sip. "Clearly, those witches don't know who I am. I've got a lot of clout and they better not forget it." Marnie realized that members knew exactly how influential the ultra-talented musician was and most were leery of establishing a friendship with her. "You girls are a God send," she slurred just a tad. She continued her tale of choral woes. "So I arranged the rendition to minimize solos... and avoid drama. God, I wish Deacon would let me require auditions. No *'whosoever will.'* Yada, yada, yada. I've lost that battle too many times."

"Despite your tiny tirade, we *all* know that the cantata will be a success," Marnie concluded. Siobhan threw an invisible kiss in her friend's direction.

"Hey, I want kisses too." Percy smirked. Marnie complied.

Monica took a gulp of wine. "I know how Deacon feels. Choose your battles wisely. Why win the battle and lose the war? If they want to sing, let 'em sing." She stared lazily into her near-empty glass and mimicked in the key of G. "Plus he knows that you will ultimately whip 'em into shape."

"Glad I don't have to deal with church drama directly." Percy joined the conversation. "I get to read about what you guys accomplish or *don't* via reams and reams of reports, memos, and calls to action. Your musicals are hugely successful for the denomination. In addition, half a dozen folks accept Christ every time. You can't do much better than that." Siobhan nodded at the affirmation.

"What about you Marnie?" Percy's right eyebrow slightly raised. "What's new with you? How is Donaldson? Is he still pimping you?" She said partially in jest. "What about that cutie, Jeremy? You still stringing him along?"

Percy was the group's pragmatist. No beating around the bush. No frills. No matter what. The same forthrightness that would make an abysmal pastor made her an exceptional administrator. Thrice divorced, Percy had twin four-year old daughters. She had recently informed the group that she was a lesbian. "Please, we've always known. A blind man would have known," Siobhan said nonchalantly. Her last marriage and divorce were amicable enough, but the other Seminary Sisters had discerned long ago that Percy always found a kindred spirit in female company and her eyes lingered on women's bums for reasons other than admiration of the female form.

"We knew you would confide in us in due season," Monica said. Although Percy wasn't seriously dating at present, they noticed how much more relaxed and at peace she was. Closed mouthed about her sexual orientation in the past, Percy now seemed empowered to share her newfound romantic exploits.

"Who would know how liberated you would become - with your navy Hugo Boss suits, and white starched button downs," Marnie teased. "Percy, you're my hero. Plus, I love that you do my taxes free!"

When Percy was in "admin mode," she was unstoppable. She had forgotten more than most people knew about accounting, legal matters, and running an enterprise. Yet Marnie loved it when she was able to unwind. "I've been dating a woman I met online. It's new, but wow, can she kiss! Her perfect breasts are perky and... the perfect mouthful." Percy's head rolled back as her friends' faces flushed, but their eyes widened with intrigue. "I'm so happy. I want each of you to feel the way I do." Marnie rubbed her friend's back.

Marnie decided to share her recent experience at Pastor Jenson's church with them, but she would avoid talking about Jeremy unless pressed. She rubbed the scarred over areas at the back of her arms. Her friends noticed, immediately made eye contact with each other, and just as quickly diverted their eyes. They never commented about Marnie's tell, but Monica was worried about her friend.

"Yeah, love. How are things?" Monica whispered in Marnie's direction.

"Well, I had a pretty interesting experience with Pastor Donaldson a few weeks ago," Marnie slowly shared.

Siobhan interrupted. "Do tell. Spit it out! Did he try to hit on you?" Although she was usually right as rain, Siobhan's weakness was a piece of good gossip.

"No." Marnie rolled her eyes. "He's flawed as a three-dollar bill, but Pastor Donaldson has never and would never do that. One of the things I admire about him is his devotion to his wife and five children. He'll bend your ear praising them." On this score, Marnie's pastor differed from so many ministers she met in seminary who were just as attracted to her ample physical gifts as they were to her spiritual ones. Marnie then recounted how Pastor Donaldson defended her during the sexist experience at New Haven Church.

"Wow! I can't believe it. Good for you. And good for ol' Donaldson," laughed Percy in a partial state of disbelief. "When is he gonna finally ordain you? You've been in training... a million years." Siobhan was noticeably silent. Like many men in their denomination, her husband vacillated on his views about women pastors. Evangelists, yes; teachers, yes; elders, yes; trustees, yes; but most of them still believed that the role of pastor was exclusively male. Marnie knew that her husband's archaic views embarrassed Siobhan.

Monica echoed, "I can't believe he had it in him. Even the most well-meaning men that I know try to avoid the elephant in the sanctuary. They don't want to talk about the sexism among their colleagues. I believe that my close male pastors truly support me, but they are hesitant to call out other male ministers when they make snide remarks about female preachers, especially those of us who are successfully growing our congregations." As the first female pastor at Johnston Temple, Monica had many sobering tales about political ploys, antics, and sometimes outright discrimination, experienced by female ministers and church leaders who only wanted equality and inclusivity. In just over five years, she had turned the once fledgling church into a moderately sized, diverse, financially stable congregation. "Sadly, I fight people inside and outside the church to get things done," Monica said. "Now that Johnston Temple can consistently pay our annual apportionment and then some, the male 'principalities in high places,' aka bishops, generally leave me alone." Although unusually optimistic, Monica's scars also made their way into the conversations with these friends.

"At least Donaldson is getting a little backbone. I remember in the not-so-distant past, how we women preachers were little more that the *Biblical Backup Singers, Holy Ghost Harem*, or the *Saintly Sidekicks* for a host of mediocre male ministers. Can I get an Amen?" Monica stood with hands raised. A litany of "Amen, Amen," and raised glasses followed. *Monica knew how to turn a phrase at the ready*, Marnie thought. That, her discerning leadership skills, and heart for people were the reasons for Monica's success in the male-dominated world of pastors.

Marnie was closest to Monica. They had spent years preaching for pennies on the "chitlin' circuit" at their pastors' friends' churches on Women's Day, Youth Day, and Pass the Plate Day. The two women had believed that many of those events were excuses for a perfunctory offering, dry cake, and a frappe. Yet they had been the most popular preachers on the circuit! Monica had given it up immediately after her appointment to Johnston Temple. Marnie had stopped because she was sick of lauds — *You are such a blessing to us! Your words inspire us! God has really anointed you!* — while being handed a check for twenty-five dollars. "Really! Twenty-five bucks for a sermon that took weeks to prepare!" she had bellowed at Monica. "I believe in paying my dues, but I still need to pay my bills." Marnie's decision to quit had been confirmed when she learned that male ministers were being paid substantially more for the same services. "We get chitlins, the boys get tenderloin!" However, the two women had remained friends and Marnie trusted Monica explicitly.

"I have to admit that Pastor Donaldson's behavior shocked me a little too," Marnie disclosed. "He was so calm, cool, and collected. I didn't even know what went on until we were driving back. I could tell by that jerk Pastor Jenson's facial expression that something was amiss, but who knew?"

Although it seemed to pain her, Monica admitted, "I admire the way Donaldson enabled that sexist Jenson to maintain his dignity, all the while putting him in his place. Talk is cheap. Actions make the difference. It's gonna take more and more male allies to push back against patriarchy in the Church." Unbeknownst to her, but to the delight of her friends, Monica was again using her preaching voice. More call and response "Amens" followed.

"You all know that I am critical of Pastor Donaldson for giving me more work and increasingly more difficult responsibilities than the men on the ministerial team. I *know* he does it. However, after that experience at New Haven, I see him in a new light. Don't get me wrong, I know he would use me up if I let him, but I saw a different side of him. Donaldson stood up for me and it really did my heart good to see it." Marnie's eyes welled up.

"Okay, he did good, but let's not go nominating him for a Nobel Peace Prize," Percy broke the stilted aura. "They still have a long way to go."

"Amen," the four friends said in unison, sipped more wine, and rested in the security of each other's company.

PART II:

Chapter 7:

Promises and Poodle Pins

The shopping duo exited in front of Brickstone Manor and followed the brightly colored signs. "Based on the online pictures and blurbs, I expect some great deals." Mrs. Hunter glanced back, beckoning Marnie to catch up. For the older woman, the adrenaline rush of negotiating was only surpassed by the unexpected find of a designer blouse, antique broach, or novel picture frame. She continued to chat over her shoulder. "I love our double dipping days. We get to find great bargains at estate sales *and* have some mother-daughter time." Marnie had inherited the knack for multitasking from her mother.

Growing up, Marnie had watched in wonder. Her mother could cook a full-course, health-conscious breakfast, get four rambunctious children and one color-blind husband dressed, and plan her own agenda without breaking a sweat! June Cleaver paled in comparison, as did other cookie-cutter television mothers. Shannon Hunter was a flesh and blood, multi-faceted woman with the skills to juggle the home front as well as the confidence to demand that her husband and children do their part. Marnie wasn't as interested in following her mother's example domestically, but she admired her ability to get things done.

As a young child, Marnie had thought her family was middle class. Etched in her memory were piano and clarinet lessons, museum trips, and vacations to her grandparent's farm. As she got older, she realized her parents' sacrifices to provide those experiences. Making ends meet with four children meant that, early on, they had struggled to be working class. "Children don't need to see behind the Wizard of Oz's curtain," Mrs. Hunter told her now adult offspring. Frequenting rummage sales had been key.

At 7:00 a.m. on Saturdays, Marnie remembered how her parents would hustle sleepy-eyed children into their station wagon. Most of the time they had squirmed in the car while their parents had searched makeshift aisles in musty garages in search for gently used, modestly priced clothes, shoes, and household items. "I hate waiting in the car." Marnie would try to stomp her tiny foot. "Can't I go in?"

"I can't have kids afoot. I must focus. Be patient, your time is coming," her mother promised. They always returned with a recliner, a table, or an old lamp that her mother refurbished and would proudly display. The maple high-back piano on which Marnie practiced Mozart had been a steal at twenty-five dollars! However, Mrs. Hunter avoided sales in nearby neighborhoods to save her children the embarrassment of possibly wearing a classmate's discarded clothes to school. Yet her sewing acumen meant an oversized woman's dress would find new life as a girl's pinafore, a pair of boy's pants, a man's button-down shirt, or six tablemats.

Although her brothers said they would rather eat worms than rummage, Mrs. Hunter was true to her word and had allowed her two teenage daughters to shop. Marnie had squirreled away her lunch money in anticipation. "Why do you waste money on clothes and purses?" Her eyes had scanned past her sister and up the shelves of books. "You're missing the real treasures." For a nickel or dime a copy, Marnie could be transported to exotic locales frequented by strong-willed sheroes and strapping heroes facing adventures and passing the time in passionate embraces. In many ways, rummage sales had fueled both Marnie's love of travel and vocabulary that later served her well in school.

In today's vernacular, rummage sales are known as estate sales. Marnie and her mother could rarely find sales, but still went to spend time together. Today they unearthed some worthy treasures. "Mom! I found a first edition James Bond novel for fifty cents thrown in that older wicker basket of encyclopedias. It has Ian Fleming's photograph and his signature too!" As they continued to wander the well-appointed, well-surveilled manor, Marnie braced for her mother's barrage of queries.

"Now *this* is an estate sale." Mrs. Hunter carried a number of silk scarves and linen tops in her size as well as a man's navy blue suit that she knew she could save from a premature death in a trash bin. "I'm so glad we could get together. You've been so busy at *that* church." Marnie recognized her mother's fishing. She knew what was coming next. "I am so very proud of what you are doing at Bethlehem. Just like your father in his day, only better. But don't tell him I said that. I'd deny it to the high heavens." She grinned and investigated a bin of antique costume jewelry. Her voice suddenly fluttered, "Oh, my, a Trifari Jelly Belly poodle pin — and for only ten dollars." Then as if a switch shifted in her brain, she stared at Marnie from head to toe.

"You aren't getting enough sleep. You're losing weight too. I don't care what those silly fashion magazines say, people need some meat on their bodies. How is Jeremy? How are things going on that front? I like him. I can tell you from personal experience; it is a challenge to find a man with the self-confidence to appreciate an educated, independent woman. Jeremy supports your ministry. He might be a keeper." Before Marnie could respond, the tirade of questions continued. "How are Monica, Siobhan, and Percy? I read a recent article about the new eldercare facility that Johnston Temple just dedicated. Monica really transformed that congregation. I heard through the grape vine that Siobhan is in the studio finishing a CD of gospel favorites. She has a gift. I could listen to her sing all day. Just enchanting. You know how I feel about Percy." Her voice trailed. Marnie learned that it was best to wait until her mother drew breath before responding; but she made a mental note of each query.

"Jeremy and I are good. He comes to church with me almost every Sunday. We are dating exclusively, but I don't know if I would call it serious." Marnie paused for her mother to interject.

"Yes, I know how cautious you are about dating. Very wise. You have too much to lose by getting hooked up with someone who is afraid to let you soar." Mrs. Hunter eyed a royal blue cashmere sweater she knew would be perfect for her eldest daughter and placed it in front of her chest to size it. However, Marnie knew that her mother was still hanging on her every utterance — word and tone.

"Jeremy supports me one hundred percent. He's more excited about my ordination than I am. I love that about him. He's so different from every person I've dated. Remember my college sweetheart, Jessie?" Marnie sneered. "I know he cared about me, but he was always competing with me. I never competed with him. I really liked the guy." She hastily stroked the back of her elbows. "That kind of competition can kill a relationship unless one of the people, usually the woman, takes second stage. I see that sometimes with Siobhan and Deacon," Marnie was now jabbering. "I choose to believe relationships exist were both partners thrive *and* support each other. Look at you and Dad." Marnie desperately needed some affirmation.

"Yes, your father is special. He was a feminist long before many women jumped on the bandwagon."

"I think Jeremy is that way too, Mom. As the young folks say, 'he's got my back.'" Marnie chuckled half-heartedly. "With him, I can just be myself. Moreover, my version of femininity never gets lost in ministry. He's special, but I don't know if marriage is for me." There. She finally admitted it. Marnie prayed and paused for the fallout.

Her mother only replied, "I know, Marn."

"What?" The young woman's mouth fell ajar.

"Marriage is not for everyone. Nor should it be. I have seen many a friend, female and male, get married because of social pressure and with devastating results. Only you will know what's right for you. And if so, only you will know when and to whom. Don't let anyone pressure you." After a long pause, Mrs. Hunter breathed. "Remember dear, it's okay to just have a special friend." *OMG. Is my mom suggesting a romantic relationship that includes sex?* Marnie forced a blush down.

"To be honest, I did make sacrifices when I got married. Not because your father required it. I just didn't have time to do all the things I planned or wanted to do. I think that happens to everyone whether married or not. For me, getting married did mean putting the needs of my family before my own. Part of maturing meant understanding the fleeting nature of time and still being excited about what you have time to do! I am very pleased with how things turned out and with more to come. Things have changed for the better for women, Marnie. It's a great sign of the times." She placed another bargain in her handcart.

"My home decorating business started as a pipe-dream. I worked out of our basement, making deliveries in that old beat-up station wagon. Now, with online sales, I have more work than I can handle. I needed a balance. Your father helped. I couldn't have done it if he was a pastor who periodically *babysat* his children and then congratulated himself for doing so. No, we built our home life together. We raised our children together. Now look at *my* children." Her lips curled high on her flawless face. "Four great people that I am proud to call my own and to call my friends. Four college graduates to boot — a minister, dentist, lawyer, and pediatrician, in no particular order," she chimed. "Yes, Marn, I am intimately involved with your father's ministry. I am proud to be his helpmate and he is certainly mine."

Marnie went on to update her mother about her friends' lives, but only those things she knew she could share. Mrs. Hunter wasn't surprised by Percy's news. "Oh, I'm glad. I was hoping she would come out sooner rather than later." The two curious shoppers spent the remainder of the morning at that one sale. Mrs. Hunter had already placed the poodle pin on her lapel. "I'll have it appraised tomorrow." They strolled into Marnie's favorite restaurant for lunch.

"Marnie, you want more. Things aren't perfect for women, but now you can have more. You don't have to slave in the shadows, living vicariously through a man. You don't have to choose between career and children. However, let's be clear. A crucial part of the equation is to choose whether you want a life partner. If you do, choose carefully. One last thing, Marn. Pastors aren't devils. Neither are they saints." Mrs. Hunter never mentioned Bethlehem Church or Rev. Donaldson. She didn't have to. Her mother's right hand brushed several stray hairs on Marnie's forehead. "Love, you will know what to do."

"Thanks." Marnie angled her head to prolong the moment.

Chapter 8:

Wedding Presents, Past, and

Future

How did I get lassoed into officiating over another wedding? Marnie eyed the rapidly receding country church in her rearview window. Dusk was fast approaching and she tried to squash the mounting concern in her gut that she got when in unfamiliar places. *It's not good for women to drive alone on strange roads at night.* Unheeded advice from: her parents; safe driving commercials; newscasters who stoically read names of missing women off teleprompters; and, seemingly every movie of the week. "I can go with you," her father had volunteered that morning.

"No, I appreciate it. Then I'd worry about you not knowing anyone there. I need to focus on leading the wedding." *I should've taken him up on his offer.* So Marnie found herself driving far enough above the speed limit to make tracks, but not far enough to draw the attention of a police car that might be hidden around an unsuspecting curve.

Although she was mentally complaining, the call from one of her seminary students honored Marnie. She taught *Religions and Its Peoples* her last semester in seminary. It was her first time teaching her own class and she was petrified. *They'll know I'm an intellectual fraud.* Instead, the twenty-five students from varied denominations, ethnicities, regions, ages, and degree programs were a joy to teach! She took great pains to treat them all equally, but Blakely Monroe found a special place in Marnie's heart.

Blakely gushed. "Dr. Hunter this and Dr. Hunter that." In response to the cloistered, rural town from which she hailed, Blakely seemed hungry for diversity. "Dr. Hunter, I grew up around people you don't walk away from. You back away from them."

Five years after the course ended, Marnie still received annual Christmas and birthday cards from Blakely. So, when she asked Marnie to officiate at her wedding, the cleric quickly agreed — even if it meant venturing to a place Blakely described as a "throwback to the movie Deliverance." Yet her love for her childhood church and her family's tight budget meant the wedding would take place in the town that Marnie was so abruptly attempting to exit.

"All these trees, shotgun houses, fields, and ponds look alike," Marnie reprimanded herself for being lost. "Where's a GPS signal when you need one. I have gas. All I needed are directions." She breathed a sigh of relief at the sight of the Gas-N-Snack from around the bend. *Please*, Marnie prayed, *let someone at this gas station know how to get to I-50!*

Jackson, the elderly man at the checkout counter, flashed a toothless grin and started pointing and rattling off directions. *Thank you, God.* Marnie looked heavenward. Just as she was scribbling the final lines, Marnie felt a chilling breeze as a figure filled her peripheral sight line. He was at least six foot four inches tall and stereotypically clad in an old wife-beater, tattered blue jeans, and dirty brown boots. In one fell swoop, he scoped out the building, ogled Marnie, and eliminated the distance between himself and the checkout counter. He slowly muttered the obvious in her direction. "You not from around here?"

The hairs on the back of her neck stood up, but she forced her lips to smile. "No, I was the minister for Blakely Monroe and Paul Stone's wedding today. Do you know them?"

After a long pause, he grumbled. "Yeah, I know their folks. Good people. Too bad their kids left for the city. They got outta here fast. Glad to see they at least have respect to come back here to marry." Marnie's smile thinned. Through his leer, she could see tobacco-stained, rotten teeth and blackened gums. "City folks even trying to take over out here." A spittle cloud floated from his mouth. Marnie made a small step backward to reestablish a comfortable distance between herself and the grizzled man.

"You a preacher?" He didn't expect Marnie to respond. "Never met a woman preacher. Don't know if I really believe in 'em, but I guess everything's okay now a' days… in the city. People don't know their place." She stepped back again, but he kept gobbling up her personal space. "Me, I like a simple life. The good ol' days. Work hard. Play hard. Me, when I'm not working, I like to hunt. Got a pair of retrievers. Black as the night. Trained 'em since they was pups. Got them bitches trained good too. They can smell possum a mile away. Full of spunk, they bring my kill right back to me. Rain, sleet, snow. It don't matter."

A tiny bead of sweat trickled down the back of Marnie's neck. She could taste a hint of bile in her throat. Her eyes darted in search of a means of escape as he continued the one-sided discourse. "Me, I love to hunt. Rabbit, duck, wild boar, possum, love to hunt me some coon too. These parts are full of coon now. Easy to pick 'em off. Once I get my bitches riled up, there's no stopping 'em. Go all night." His eyes glazed over as he spoke nostalgically.

"This so-called diversity thing is really taking off. Me Too, You Too, whatever it's called. You people are really moving up though," he continued. "Everywhere I look now. On TV, the news — women. And even immigrants and minorities." He cackled. "Truth be told, I don't mind you ladies too much, though, as long as you got big racks. Still miss the good ol' days." His bite dragged, but it met its mark. Marnie yearned to make this place a distant memory, but the fire shut up in her bones swelled.

"Well, the good old days weren't as good and aren't as old for some folks as they are for others." Marnie's tiny hands instinctively made fists. She gulped, prepared to pounce verbally. *I'll give him a piece of my mind. I won't miss it, and he sorely needs it.*

"Hey Big Ed, Big Ed Fountain. How's Lil' Ed doing? I don't think I've seen him in a few weeks! What's he up to? I swear that boy has grown a foot every time I see 'im." Jackson's queries momentarily averted the burly man's leer in Marnie's direction. His expression softened as he recounted his son's growth spurt, recent sports accomplishments, and all around genius. Marnie knew that the questions were a Hail Mary pass to provide her time to escape, if she chose to do so. She did.

Marnie darted past the beat-up red pick-up truck standing between her and freedom. She jumped in her car, locked the doors, and strapped on her seatbelt. Her hands shook as she started the car and turned out of the lot. *God bless you, Jackson!* At least Marnie now knew she was driving in the right direction. Only about twenty more miles to the interstate. She turned on her favorite CD and crooned along. "Jesus, Savior, pilot me. Over life's tempestuous sea; Unknown waves before me roll, Hiding rock and treacherous shoal. Chart and compass come from Thee; Jesus, Savior, pilot me." The road seemed to meander with the tune. "I-50!" She yelled aloud.

Marnie was about to turn onto the interstate when she saw smoke billowing from the nearby ditch to her right. It was officially dark, but she could make out a truck — a beat-up red pick-up truck. *It must have slid off the road and fallen into the narrow embankment*, she surmised. The impact slightly concaved its middle. She couldn't tell which dents were due to the accident and which were the result of age and neglect. The vehicle was lying partly on its right side. Tiny gold and red sparks shot upward, momentarily lighting the darkness. Marnie slammed on the brake and careened off the road a short distance behind the accident.

As Marnie dashed toward the driver's side of the truck, the stench of exhaust smoke, soot, fumes, gasoline, and charred flesh grew thicker, chocking her throat, and burning her eyes. Wiping her eyes only worsened the stinging pain as the heat spread from the ignited vehicle. She reached the door. Relief. *The window is down.* Marnie's eyes widened in disbelief. She could see the burly outline of Big Ed slumped in the driver's seat, his body hunched slightly forward, and trapped in the fiery tin can! Marnie futilely yanked to open the door and reached through the open window to accomplish the same goal, but to no avail. She touched the crumpled driver to find a pulse. *Please God let him be alive!* She didn't know how she was going to get him out of the impending inferno. *Marnie, handle one problem at a time.*

Big Ed gradually opened his bloodshot eyes; his mouth soon followed. Just above a whisper, he sluggishly growled, "Hel, hel, help, help me… cunt."

Marnie's body reeled backward unsure of whether her profuse sweating was due to the growing flames or the man. Her feet seemed lodged in the heated earth near the mangled truck. The fuel smell intensified and smoke continued to attack her eyes and nose. Marnie could still see the poison in Big Ed's eyes, intermingled with blood dribbling down the left side of his face. The slur drove her several feet from the driver's door; the distance seemed like a chasm. Yet she could still hear the wounded man hurling a barrage of epithets and demands in her direction. She stood immobile in the black, gray, gold, and red-hot space. She tried to command her body to tread those requisite steps to the dangerous, trapped man. Then Marnie heard an almost inaudible groan followed by a squeaky stream of pants and cries emanating from the passenger side of the truck. A snip of blond and copper tinged hair was barely visible next to the man's heavily tattooed right arm. Marnie gasped. *Lil' Ed was also trapped inside the twisted metal!*

She dashed around the front of the truck. The passenger side window was up and the door locked. She desperately beat at the window with her hands, but it wouldn't respond to her physical entreat. "Please God, help me," Marnie cried aloud. "Help me!" She mustered all of her energy and hit the center of the glass squarely with her right elbow. Fragments and slivers fell away. Without noticing the line of shards jutting up from the window rim, Marnie reached inside and dislodged the tiny, whimpering child. He wasn't wearing a seatbelt either so she attempted to drag Lil' Ed through the vacant window frame.

The boy either was in shock or passed out; he felt like dead weight. Marnie struggled to free him. The glass shards pulled at the flesh on her elbows as she cupped the almost lifeless body. Her efforts etched lines of scars on her arms in their wake that Marnie would forever carry. She winced but tried to make sure Lil' Ed's body wasn't exposed to the broken glass. When he flinched, she knew she hadn't been successful, but she also knew he was alive! Marnie and Lil' Ed would now have matching physical reminders of that fateful night.

She hurriedly lugged the boy a safe distance away from the burning truck and gingerly laid him on the ground. Her attempts at CPR were rudimentary, but when Lil' Ed began to cough and squirm, Marnie was relieved. "Shhh, shh, it's going to be all right." She stroked blood and soot from his brow. "Everything is going to be all right."

"Where's my Daddy?" the boy whimpered. "Where's Daddy?" Marnie faced a bigger problem. How to get the massive, irate man free.

"Don't worry, son. Don't worry," she cooed. "Be still right here. I'm going to help your daddy." Could she keep that promise?

Just as Marnie rushed back toward the driver's door, several thunderous booms erupted as the truck exploded and flames shot high into the night sky! The intensity of the blast blew her to the ground; she scrambled backward across the damp ground and covered her eyes for fear of the flames that continued to flick from the wreckage. Marnie's mouth hung open in horror. Were those Ed's screams amidst the roar of the fire or was her imagination fueled by the night wind? Was he still futilely calling out for help from the smoldering pile of debris? Marnie wailed. She welcomed the quiet calm of darkness that gradually enveloped her as she fainted on the warm gravel.

The confused minister awoke in the emergency room of the small, rural hospital. Several doctors and nurses scurried around her and the other figure on a nearby gurney. *How long was she out?* "Can you hear me, Miss? Do you know your name?" The doctor was checking her heart rate with his stethoscope.

"Yes, yes. Marnie, Marnie Hunter." The medical team thwarted her attempts to sit up.

"Please lie still, Ma'am. You have a concussion, several broken ribs, and severe bruises and burns on your arms. Please try to lie still!" Marnie obeyed, but questioned. "Where's the little boy? I need to know where he is. Is he all right?" She couldn't bear to think that she failed both father and son.

The second physician calmly said, "He's fine. They're caring for him over there."

The slow beep of a hospital monitor reassured her somewhat of Lil' Ed's status.

"Please tell me... his wounds?" she continued. She didn't ask about Big Ed. Marnie feared that answer.

"Don't worry, Miss. Hunter. Edward is doing just fine. His injuries are similar to yours: two broken ribs, scrapes, burns, bruises, but also serious smoke inhalation. He's a real trooper. His mother is on her way." He paused and gazed warmly at Marnie. "You're a hero. He wouldn't have made it out without you. Now relax. The pain medication we gave you will take effect soon. You need to rest. We took the liberty to notify the contact person listed on the back of your driver's license. I'm sure he will be here when you wake up. So please relax."

"What about the man? Tell me what happened to him." No one responded as the sedative soon forced Marnie back into darkness.

The accident was five years ago. The doctors reported that Marnie repressed certain parts of the experience. To her, she remembered every detail, word, emotion, smell, sound, and sensation. Marnie couldn't excise them. The scars on her elbows and arms were constant reminders of what she had and hadn't done. Marnie woke up screaming many nights after the accident with the smell of chard flesh anew in her nostrils. As time passed, the nightmares ebbed, but the guilt and uncertainty dragged like a ball and chain.

Chapter 9:

Whosever Will, Let *Her* Come!

"No pastor or denominational Governing Board can decide whether you're qualified to be a preacher. God already decided that," said her father, his hands firmly planted on each of her shoulders. "You don't need anyone to validate you. God did that as well."

Marnie gazed at him warmly. "I know I have a pretty good reputation at Bethlehem Church and Pastor Donaldson will vouch for me. I still want to be ordained. It's about the calling."

"I can relate. It was a life-changing rite of passage for me."

"I'm ready, Dad. It's been over five years since I graduated from seminary. I know it's a rigorous process. I know that Governing Board includes some of the highest-ranking people in CC. However, they have to ordain me. They just have to!" She rubbed an elbow through her favorite exercise jersey. He noticed.

Five male and two female senior clerics were responsible for ordination oversight. They shaped the future leadership of the denomination. Although several local pastors were responsible for training and mentoring, the board would evaluate the twenty-paged written exam before candidates could proceed to a series of formal training sessions. It would also oversee the final oral exam for the fortunate few who made it that far.

"I know I can serve in most church capacities without getting ordained. Many preachers do. No stigma or shame. For me, like you, this vetting is everything!" They were silent for the rest of their walk. As she waved her father's car out of the parking lot, Marnie thought that maybe talking things through with Monica during dinner later that night would help. She stroked her right elbow again.

Several hours and multiple outfit and shoe iterations later, Marnie sat across from her best friend for an early dinner. "Thanks for dragging me out tonight. I exercised with Dad this morning, but I've been pining about ordination since then," admitted Marnie.

"I thought you might need a night out with all this ordination stuff." Monica stole a fried oyster from her best friend's appetizer plate.

"Thanks. You read my mind. I'm losing it." She fingered the rim of her water glass.

"Been there, done that. You remember how stressed I was during my process a few years back? You were an anchor. Now I can return the favor. Here try this." She reached a fork of escargot toward Marnie's welcoming lips.

"Mmm... tasty." Marnie's concerns were temporarily lost in the salty flavors of the succulent snails. "I'm not afraid of the process. I'm just tired of waiting. I feel like I'm being led on." She slammed her left palm on the restaurant table then glanced around self-consciously.

"You're preaching to the choir." Monica tilted her wine glass.

"Plus, there are so few ordained female clergy in our denomination. Only about one hundred women among thousands of men. Abysmal. I think it's more to do with patriarchy than the caliber of female seminary graduates. Breaking gender barriers would also make it possible for more women to hold key denominational positions. I want to be in that number."

"Here, here," Monica agreed. "Think about the two women board members. Both are pastors of two of the largest, most financially stable congregations in the CC. Both earned PhDs rather than the Doctor of Ministry degree common among male clergy. Each penned numerous books on more religious topics to count. Don't get me wrong, the other board members are impressive, but they pale in comparison." *You go, girls!* Marnie mentally cheered.

Even later that night, with both her stomach and spirit refilled, Marnie thought about the ordination process. A score of eighty-five out of one hundred points would qualify her to participate in the training activity that included performing mock funerals, weddings, baby dedications, and baptisms. The board automatically dismissed candidates who didn't pass these tests. To make matters worse, they wouldn't know their assignments until the day of the test! Therefore, she'd have to be ready to lead all four rituals. *Jesus, take the wheel!* However, her father reminded her during their stroll that very morning, "These are all critical church rituals that all clergy should perform well." Based on a combination of poor written test scores, conflicting schedules, and fear of the unknown, the group of seven candidates from Bethlehem Church alone dwindled to four, three females and one male. Albeit inconsistently, Pastor Donaldson had helped them prepare for the Q&A activities, mock tests, and oral exam. "I've got to focus. No distractions. No Big Ed in my head… not now." As if speaking it aloud would make it so.

The following week, Marnie eyed the crisp, white envelope on her coffee table for several hours before finally ripping it open. She passed her written exams with flying colors! Pastor Donaldson was unable to contain himself during their next team meeting. "It's a confidential process, but I thought you'd like to know how impressed the Governing Board was with your test scores. You're the youngest candidate *and* the youngest woman in the cohort." *I bet you took credit. Think positive, girl.* "I'm a proud pastor. Are you ready for the mock presentations?" Her heart sank.

Marnie impressed the board later that week as she officiated over a mock wedding ceremony. "Loved your special touches and wedding remarks specific for the 'interracial couple' we assigned you. Just beautiful! You effortlessly addressed every aspect of the wedding," one board member spoke and clapped.

"Yes, yes. I appreciated your strategic use of humor and practical examples. Weddings don't have to be so formal and boring. It's a celebration!" A second judge interjected. "Let's see how you handle a funeral," he said, channeling Dastardly Whiplash.

Marnie didn't disappoint. Her mock funeral service for a fictitious infant who died of leukemia brought board members and candidates alike to tears. Candidates could only bring their ministerial handbooks because part of the test was to scour the church site for makeshift items for the assigned event. *A scavenger hunt too! You can do this.* Marnie willed herself. She dashed through several cluttered storage rooms to create the things needed to convey a child's home-going service. Her dormant Super Saint skills emerged. Two boxes and a velvet tablecloth became a small casket; several floral arrangements were substituted for condolence wreaths. Volunteers served as the grieving family.

This particular event might have seemed a bit macabre to some candidates, but Marnie had an affinity for people who were experiencing grief. *I know how they feel.* She recalled when her younger brother, Henry, had died. She had been seven; he had been five. The pain and feelings of impotency were still acute. His tiny body had wasted away from leukemia too. Moreover, the trauma about Lil' Ed still loomed large. *Maybe I should ask for another assignment?* She thought. *No, stick it out.* She did. Marnie chose the appropriate songs, bible passages, and litany. She spared nothing. She selected two event-specific hymns, "Jesus Loves the Little Children" and "When We All Get to Heaven," as well as Matthew 19:13-17 that describes Jesus' special relationship with children and Psalms 23 about God as a comforting shepherd. Marnie knew the funeral wasn't real, but she sensed that in a way, God was giving her a chance to say goodbye to Henry as an adult. However, could she reconcile the Lil' Ed situation?

Written exam done. Check. Mock trials done. Check. Marnie was two for two. Yet she couldn't shake the aching feeling that the overall ordination process smacked of bias. As usual, Monica was her sounding board. "Yes, your all-knowing sidekick has the answers you seek." She grinned a bit too wide.

"Stop it. I'm serious. I can't help but notice the latitude given to some of the male trainees, their pedestrian responses to questions, and excused absences. They aren't taking this process seriously. Especially the legacies. They act so entitled, like this process is just a minor roadblock between them and a pastorate with big bucks!"

"Seen it, sadly, before." Monica moved to wrap her friend in a bear hug, but Marnie wasn't ready to be warm and fuzzy.

"To make matters worse, they're dumb as stumps. You can't be a mediocre diva!"

"I know it's a cliché, but take it one day at a time. I remember that ten-pound binder of readings. Take it one page at a time." Now Marnie was ready for that hug; Monica complied.

The candidates got over their competitive tensions and decided to form a weekly study group. They quizzed each other, debated biblical and theological topics, and talked about practical ministerial responsibilities. Did a Minister of Music, youth minister, mission's leader, or church counselor need special skills? What are the skills all ministers need? Was it possible to measure effectiveness? The cadre of young clergy toiled individually and collectively and grew closer as a result.

On one particular evening, a larger than usual group of trainees gathered to study. Joe Lewis and

Frank drove in from Jonesville. Janie and Mary were from a local church in the city. Bonita, Clara, and Marnie were from Bethlehem. Rodney Rollins, the bishop's nephew, just returned from a fraternity convention and decided to grace them with his presence. *Oh, what joy*, Marnie smirked. *Think good things. Only positive energy.* She wasn't alone in her thoughts. Frank cupped his hands like a bullhorn.

"Dude, love that Armani Collezioni suit, but you might wanna buy a better watch. You're forty-five minutes late!" Rodney took the laughter in stride. Between bites of pizza and potato chips, Frank started the discussion. "In Matthew 22:21, just exactly what did Jesus mean when He said, 'Render unto Caesar the things that are Caesar's, and unto God the things that are God's'? Why would he even suggest that believers support any part of the oppressive Roman government? Was he acknowledging their sovereignty? If so, does that undermine His sovereignty? Sounds like defeatism to me."

Joe Lewis interrupted. "Jesus wasn't suggesting defeat by any stretch of the imagination! He was telling believers to both respect the government or earthly authority and recognize that it has some influence over our lives."

"I agree. Christ wanted His followers to challenge any system that was being elevated over Him, but He still wanted them to remember that the government was real. He knew very well that Rome was oppressive," Bonita interjected.

"Although the Romans thought Christ and His followers were on a political mission, they were wrong. Jesus' mission wasn't political in the way we think about politics," Clara noted while smashing several chips into her mouth.

"Jesus was all about love. Remember, in verses 37-40 of that same chapter, He told the people, 'You shall love the Lord your God with all your heart, and with all your soul, and with all your mind. This is the greatest and first commandment. A second is like it: You shall love your neighbor as yourself. On these two commandments hang all the law and the prophets,'" said Janie.

"Check out the quote, verbatim, coming from *Rev.* Janie. *Somebody's* been studying her bible. Trying to get ready for the Big Day," teased Frank. "The Governing Board won't trip her up."

"*Somebody* better start studying if *he* wants to be in the number," she retorted much to the group's amusement. "As I was saying before I was so rudely interrupted." Janie winked toward Frank. "So, applying the Great Commandments, if you love other people, you will be okay doing your part to ensure that things on earth, like the government, function properly."

"People, please, remember that the Romans were tyrants. Jesus despised the way they treated their citizens, especially how they mistreated Jews. Remember the poverty and inequality. Jesus wasn't always feeding five thousand folks here and three thousand there for his health. These weren't parlor tricks to amuse the gathering masses. People were hungry!" Rodney pushed his way into the dialogue. Marnie didn't like his vibe, but she admitted that he made a good point.

"Jesus' mission was all about reconciliation — reconciling humanity back to God. Getting us back in the right relationship with God. The Romans were nervous and jealous because He was able to draw large crowds. They thought He was trying to overthrow the government. They couldn't even fathom the scope of His mission." Her peers nodded at Marnie's remark.

"I agree but remember that Jesus' ministry was spiritual *and* practical. Caesar's face was on their currency, not Jesus'." Frank threw in that remark for good measure.

Marnie responded. "What are you talking about, Frank? Jesus saw the corruption in the government. He was trying to get His followers to open up their eyes. Yes, His focus was on agape love, but that does not mean that Christ didn't want to turn the entire world upside down!"

"Yeah," said Clara. "I believe that Jesus was really saying, 'give the Romans what is rightly theirs, but by the way, nothing is theirs because everything belongs to God — so people, you better recognize!'" They all laughed at the usually quiet trainee's unexpected use of slang. They agreed that her comment was on target. Marnie winked at Clara and passed her friend a half-empty pizza box. Feeling somehow outdone by his unassuming colleague, Rodney seemed compelled to speak, even if only to affirm Clara. "Overall, Christ wanted people to have their priorities in order. Yes, be able to live in this world, but not of this world."

Bonita nodded. "Yes. Yes. Because if we love God first and really love our neighbors the way we love ourselves, we wouldn't have to worry about corrupt governments, poverty, discrimination, sexism and all the other isms in the world."

"It seems hard for a lot of folks to put God first. And how can we love other people when some of us don't even love ourselves?" questioned Joe Lewis.

"So true, but that's another theological debate for another day," Rodney remarked, looking at his watch and the empty food containers and cups now strewn around the group.

"That's what makes what we do, what we are trying to do and preparing to do better, so important. It's our responsibility to make sure people understand these truths. We have to tell people what Christ did for them and what God expects us to do for and with each other." Marnie's voice trailed off and the entire group stilled at the sheer magnitude of the mission they accepted.

"Amen... so true... you're so right." They echoed. Someone asked Clara to give the closing prayer. Then each cleric, sufficiently girded up spiritually and physically, strolled to their respective cars.

The group of initially frightened trainees slowly realized that they weren't competing for a select number of slots but preparing for a lifetime of service. There was room at the cross for them all. Marnie's feelings vacillated between preparedness and a mild case of imposture's syndrome. Most of all, she had a nagging feeling that the experience with Big and Lil' Ed somehow made her unworthy for the honor of ordination. The tracks of scars on her arms and elbows were more irritating lately. Maybe it was her imagination.

Chapter 10:

Colliding Shadows in the

Distance

"I've been patient, Marnie, but I have to be honest, I'm feeling neglected. We rarely see each other. When we do, you are preoccupied with church work. What gives? I don't mind sharing you, but lately, I'm only getting crumbs, scraps… sloppy seconds… and believe me, I'm really hungry." Marnie chuckled at Jeremy's creative use of metaphor and strategic pauses. *He has mad preacher skills*, she grinned slightly. Jeremy caught a glimpse of her facial expression, but without the benefit of its complimentary origins. It only made matters worse.

"Oh, so you think this is funny? It's funny that I call and call and you *never* return my calls? It's funny that we haven't gone out in over three weeks? You disappear without telling me. You are thin as a rail. Yes, it's hilarious that I've almost forgotten how you feel in my arms. Let's not forget that, if and when we are intimate, my tongue and I are usually doing all the work! Yes, Marnie, I'm in stiches!" Jeremy cocked his head to the left the way he always did when cross.

It was a miracle that Marnie had ever met Jeremy. Monica had said it best during a Seminary Sister night out. "Guys don't make passes at girl's who wear glasses... because guys are asses." The levity of the quip had been lost on its gravity. Marnie had initially thought her friend was being myopic, but over the years, she had found some truth in her point.

"You're one to complain." Percy had pushed back that night. "Your man lived most of his life abroad. He's immune to most U.S. rules about gender."

Marnie had informed Monica, palms forward, "Yeah, I'd love to fall in love with a Frenchman like your Sebastian. They're so mysterious and affable." Monica's eyes had twinkled. Memories aside, at present, Marnie was on a collision course toward Jeremy.

Marnie had dated the same person throughout high school. It had been an unexpected union between nerd and jock. "I like having a *smart* girlfriend. You improve my academic cred and I improve your street cred." Keith had stuck out his chest. Neither had really cared about what other people thought. However, the distance at separate colleges had eventually pulled them apart. College guys, even really smart ones, had seemed put off by Marnie. *Why should I care about guys who only see me as competition rather than a potential partner?* Time and a bit of wisdom had caused the introvert to realize the value of male companionship. Once Marnie had become a minister, she often felt like a leper!

She dressed conservatively, attended lots church events, and worked at a church so the few guys she attracted tended to be ultra conservative. All they wanted to do was settle down and start pro-creating. Then they got to know Marnie. Firm in her faith, she was comfortable questioning the bible, theology, and everything in between. *Too liberal, too many opinions, just too much!* Needless to say, most of them eventually ran screaming from the room. *Too Bad. Their loss.* Moreover, although Marnie's figure was well toned and curvy, she didn't fit traditional images of female beauty either. She purposely kept her shoulder length raven hair cropped short. Minimal make-up because it took too long to put it on and take it off, she surmised. "I'm just more comfortable wearing slacks and flat shoes than pencil skirts and pumps," Marnie had informed her parents about her fashion sense long ago.

"Be yourself, dear. You are still striking. People who met you never forget it." Mrs. Hunter had looked her daughter up and down and winked. Marnie had imagined herself walking through a crowd of men and watching them topple like bowling pins! "Am I ever going to get any grandchildren?" Her mother had added only half in jest. Marnie had smiled and rolled her eyes.

Then Marnie met Jeremy. Her quirks, solitary nature, and his laid-back style made for a perfect match. It was a fluke that their paths had even crossed. Marnie had practically lived at the nearby library where Jeremy worked while completing her Master's thesis. The miles of dusty books had felt like home. If she had walked down another aisle that last night, they would never have met. Jeremy believed it was fate and loved to regale anyone about it who would listen.

"I wasn't supposed to even be working that evening, but I swapped shifts with a colleague at the last minute. Then I saw this vision with thick-rimmed glasses and dark, disheveled hair wearing slightly baggy, well-worn jeans. She was like a sexy schoolteacher. She floated down the aisle like an angel." No matter how Marnie's face flushed, Jeremy would always continue. "My interest was further piqued when I saw the books she juggled in her tiny arms: Gutierrez's *A Theology of Liberation*; *Womanist Justice, Womanist Hope* by **Emilie Townes**; Weber's *The Protestant Ethic and the Spirit of Capitalism*; and teetering atop the pile, **Dubois'** *Darkwater*. I just had to meet her!"

Marnie too had been intrigued by a six foot four, two-hundred-pound, male librarian. As she had eyed him lumbering towards her, books in hand and a pencil behind his right ear, she had known that they couldn't pass in the narrow stacks at the same time. They were sure to collide. They both had turned sideways, but their bodies still brushed. Electric. Jeremy had admitted, "After walking by her, I raced to the checkout counter and demanded to work there for the remainder of the evening. The rest, as they say, is history."

At present, all Marnie wanted was a quiet Saturday evening with Jeremy. After several cancelled dates due to her frantic work schedule, she looked forward to spending time with him in front of the fire, eating pizza, and cuddling. Instead, Jeremy turned it into an opportunity to vent.

Marnie could hear Jeremy's rants, but they began to sound like the incongruent tones of Ms. Donovan, Charlie Brown's teacher. She initially planned to simply simper and address Jeremy's charges with a wink, hug, and some appropriate petting. Not now. Marnie was learning to push back against pushy men.

"*Poor Jeremy*. He's feeling neglected! He's feeling put upon. *Jeremy* wants Marnie's undivided attention!" She knew he hated it when she spoke about him in the third person. Marnie continued pushing. "Why are you complaining? I'm here. I'm here, right here, and right now. We're both busy people. I don't complain about our limited time together. Don't act like I'm the only one who has cancelled one of our dates." Jeremy looked down at his hands. Marnie continued, now above a whisper. "I've missed you. I miss you all the time. However, you know how I feel about ministry. You *knew* I was a minister when you met me. What I do, who I am, is not about money, power, or status. This is my calling!" Her hands shook.

"Oh… and in the matter of our depressing sex life. I'm so very sorry you are unfulfilled." Marnie lowered her eyes as her cheeks reddened. "You knew about my limited sexual experiences. Remember again, I'm a preacher! You know how I was raised! I even confided in you about my Super Saint experience as a child at church and how it messed with my head. I can't believe you'd throw this up in my face. Oh, and that remark about your tongue. How could you? I thought we turned the corner in a big way. I give as good as I get… and that was a huge step for me!" Marnie refused to cry. She wouldn't let him see her cry.

Although she wouldn't admit it, especially to Jeremy at that moment, she was exhausted from another day at Bethlehem. The work, conflict, and tensions were unrelenting. Pastor Donaldson seemed oblivious to both the situation and the toll it was taking on her spiritually, physically, and emotionally. Jeremy wasn't making it any better. *Yet another man making demands on her.* "I gotta go!" she shouted as she rubbed the back of her right elbow, snatched her coat from the nearby chair, and burst out the front door into the quiet night.

Marnie knew too many narcissistic, male ministers. The power they wielded in congregants only worsened their sense of entitlement. Jeremy was different. Or so she thought. Was she naïve to think he was without self-centered tendencies? Were her father and Pastor James the only men she could really trust? She hustled down the driveway toward her car. *The bible says a man who finds a good wife finds a good thing. So single women shouldn't be trying to find men; men should be searching for us.* The verse provided little comfort in the chilly night air.

Jeremy loved her. Marnie knew it. He wanted to take their relationship to the next stage. She knew that too. He supported her work, applauded her accomplishments, and never considered her a threat to his masculinity. Jeremy wanted to marry her. He would even wait until then to have sex. Yet Marnie continued to push him away. Yes, some of the long periods between their dates were her doing. *Keep him at bay. Hold on to your independence, your heart, and your secrets as long as you can.* Marnie felt comfortable advising single people and couples, gay or straight, about abstinence, sex, or options in between. Why couldn't she practice what she preached? Now it might be too late.

That night, Marnie confided in Monica about her spat with Jeremy. "My greatest fear is being like couples I knew who get married, refurbish an old, charming Tudor together, and after raising children, realize they never really knew each other at all. Then they divorce and marry their soul mate. I would rather wait for that second guy." Monica realized that she was there to listen. "I also want to avoid the fate of people who barely escaped bad marriages and spend the rest of their lives licking their wounds." If she was honest, Marnie found something almost sacred in being single. She wasn't interested in a marriageable male. No need for a protector or provider. "Sometimes it seems like women are looking for good men to protect them from bad ones." Monica only nodded. Then Big Ed invaded her thoughts. She wasn't ready to share him with Monica. Not yet.

Marnie respected the married life of women like Monica and Siobhan, but she didn't envy it. Sometimes after drinking more wine than expected, Siobhan let it slip that she tempered her abilities and successes sometimes for the sake of her husband. Unlike her talented friend, Marnie knew that she would never have to stand in Jeremy's shadow. He would always encourage her to shine in her own way. Although she really wanted to and they always said good night on the telephone before bed, Marnie didn't call Jeremy that night. He didn't call her either. Sunday would be another busy day. She tossed, turned, and tried to wish herself to sleep. No such luck.

Chapter 11:

Eclipses, Silhouettes, and

Muted Flickers

The haggard young woman stumbled along the dark, dank, deserted alley, darting between abandoned cars, strewn trash, and partially decayed corpses. She was desperate for shelter. Smoke stung her pupils; her clothes were torn and filthy. She could hear her heart thumping in her chest, its thuds only competed with rumbles from a stomach neglected by food. Her throat was tight and parched. Physically and emotionally spent, she commanded her legs to keep moving. If she expected to survive the night, she had to find a safe haven from both the throng of reanimated corpses roaming the city tearing asunder everyone and everything in their path as well as from angst-ridden survivors searching for food and shelter by any means necessary. The woman saw her reflection in a broken, dusty stained-glass window of an abandoned church. It was Marnie!

She stopped to catch her breath when she heard the rising cacophony of grunts, moans, and hisses from the fast-approaching horde of undead. She faintly recognized some of the rhythmically writhing figures. Marnie fell back in horror at the disfigured, misshapen faces of Big Ed, Lil' Ed, Rev. Chet, and MOBs from the churches from her past! Even Pastor Donaldson's body staggered toward her, arms flailing, and mouth cruelly contorted and stained with blood. She tried to escape, but the lifeless swarm engulfed her with their decomposing fingers, hands, and teeth. Her blood curdling screams were lost as her body was ripped apart.

Marnie yanked herself out of the bad dream! She was drenched from head to toe in perspiration. *Arms, legs, feet, all present and accounted for,* she hastily appraised. The sounds, smells, feelings, and sights were so real! Was her work now invading her sub-conscious? Could she find any peace? Marnie glared at her alarm clock. *6:46 a.m. I've got to get to Bethlehem by 8:00 a.m.*

Bethlehem Church wasn't a megachurch by any stretch of the imagination. However, with over one thousand members, twenty-five weekly programs, and a staff of thirteen ministers over which Marnie presided, organizing Sunday services was crucial. This didn't mean that Pastor Donaldson didn't ad-lib as led by the Holy Spirit or that the choir director couldn't repeat a particularly moving song. Yet they planned every detail of that experience.

"People come to church to meet the Lord," Pastor Donaldson challenged during ministry meetings. "Things must be done decently and in order." Yes, he was paraphrasing 1 Corinthians 14:40, but they all got the point. As the Associate Minister, Marnie made sure

Sundays went off without a hitch. However, with an 8:30 a.m. worship service, nine Sunday school classes at 9:30 a.m., and an 11:00 a.m. worship service, not to mention running children, late ushers, and absent deacons, Marnie's hands were more than full. *They runneth over.*

"Everything we do should point to the invitation. How glorious when someone accepts Christ as his Lord and Savior or re-dedicates herself to Christ." Marnie challenged the ministers under her purview. She also focused on church growth and the caliber of evangelism at Bethlehem. "We don't want anyone to miss out on a relationship with God." Bethlehem had grown fourfold. Their social services to the poor, elderly, incarcerated, and homeless were well respected. Despite his shortcomings, Pastor Donaldson's finger was on the pulse of the community. "I want Bethlehem to be a safe haven for church and community members twenty-four hours a day, seven days a week." Now if only its' Associate Minister could find such sanctuary.

Marnie's role also meant mediating between MOBs who wanted hymns and "fire and brimstone" sermons and the growing younger contingency drawn to gospel music, practical sermons, and liturgical dancing. During the ministerial debriefing at the end of each Sunday, she recapped. "Look at the number of youth, teenagers, and young couples in worship today. Pastor Donaldson's sermons about social justice really draw them. Sunday school numbers are up too." She breathed a sigh of relief. Common sense changes like snacks during bible studies, tutoring for children and youth while their parents rehearsed in the choir, youth step teams, dance ministries, poetry slams, and Sunday continental breakfasts attracted diverse people to this once fledgling congregation.

Pastor Donaldson interjected. "Congrats everyone for another great Sunday experience. I'm especially proud of our continued ability to attract and retain men. These aren't just CME men — Christmas, Mother's Day, and Easter." Several clergy smothered their snickers with their hands. "They're active men and it didn't happen overnight."

A year earlier, Pastor Donaldson had proposed that Bethlehem hold one Sunday worship service from 10:00 a.m. until 11:30 a.m. during football season. "Why are we competing with afternoon sports when we don't have to? We're actually trying to attract men." He had tried to rally the troops.

"Preposterous. Is Bethlehem a church or a social club? The church is supposed to change the world, not vice versa!" the MOBs had decried. Several had transferred their membership to a "real church" when Bethlehem started to host weekly sports events on its jumbo-tron televisions and sponsor Super Bowl parties. In addition, Marnie had heard through the ministerial grapevine that Pastor Donaldson had become the butt of jokes among some local pastors.

"Bear with me, Christians. Let's try this for a year. If it doesn't work, we can go back to our original schedule." It had worked! Marnie and the other ministers had been behind the scenes to ensure it did. This had meant performing focus groups with men inside and outside the church about their needs and interests as well as marketing directly to them strategic using fliers, social media, and neighborhood canvasing.

Even the right snacks had been crucial. Chicken wings, pizza, chips, popcorn — yes! Rice cakes and humus — no! Marnie had left no stone unturned. Soon church and non-church events had begun to attract more men. Women had followed. Even the MOBs had started wearing NFL tee shirts on Sports Sunday. A rumor had even suggested strain in Mothers Johnson and Briar's once close relationship because of a Rose Bowl upset!

Yet members never knew that Marnie had given the idea. She had suggested to Pastor Donaldson that the church implement demographic-specific outreach, starting with men's activities. Despite the Seminary Sisters' taunts, "Stop falling on your sword, woman," Marnie had decided to take one for the team. Pastor Donaldson had been grateful for her commitment and confidences. In addition, clergy who had once laughed at him were now enviously instituting similar programs. *Cool, there is plenty of room at the cross.* Marnie had witnessed the slow deaths of too many churches clutching archaic traditions despite aging memberships and dwindling funds. Marnie believed that the hearts of the leaders at Bethlehem, including Pastor Donaldson, were in the right place. So she continued to toil.

Pastor Donaldson closed the meeting with more affirmations. He clapped and everyone mimicked. Marnie closed the meeting with prayer. *Whew, I made it.* Pastor Donaldson squeezed her tightly before driving off to dinner with his family. Marnie was about to do the same, when several of the elderly women, Mothers Matheson and Peters, and Sister Right, sauntered over and positioned themselves between Marnie and her car. *Too late to escape.*

Mother Masterson began, "Minister Hunter, thank you so much for all that you do here at Bethlehem. Service was especially uplifting today. The pastor's sermon was inspirational. My, didn't the Children's Choir just bless our hearts. They're little angels." They were unaware of the multiple fires Marnie had put out, including breaking up a fight between two of those *little angels*. Marnie heard the frenzied buzz of her internal MOB alert.

"We must speak to you about an urgent matter," Mother Peters commanded.

The final member of the trio, Sister Right, purred. "Because the matter involves the women of the church, Pastor Donaldson directed us to you. We know you are probably tired after such a long day, but this matter just can't wait." *Wow, I can't believe he threw me under the bus! He's probably already enjoying dinner.*

"Ladies, how might I help you?" They marched back to her office.

"We are aware of the pastor's push toward attracting and retaining youth and young adults. Scripture clearly says, whosoever will, let him come. We are so proud of the growing number of young folks who now attend Bethlehem. Few Sundays pass when our pews aren't overflowing." Marnie did not trust Mother Masterson's syrupy statements. "But we have to do something about their inappropriate attire, especially the young women. Every Sunday I am increasingly chagrinned and flabbergasted by the exposed skin that I am forced to see."

"So true, so true," said her minion, Sister Right. "The short skirts, low necklines, and sleeveless dresses are just an affront!" Mother Peters nodded halfheartedly as her friend carped.

"Christians must do things decently and in order. That means wearing appropriate church attire! My stomach turns every time I see some of these girls enter God's house! Believe me, He is displeased!" Sister Right eyed Marnie up and down. "Just look at you, Minister Hunter. You always dress in a godly way. You never wear sleeveless dresses to church." She grinned cheekily. *You couldn't be more wrong about my reasons. You don't know my secret.*

"And how will they know unless we teach them?" Mother Masterson exegeted scripture to serve her purposes. "We want to recommend that the church purchase lap scarves and shawls to distribute to young women as they enter the sanctuary." The older woman continued, "We would notify the ushers of an offending young lady and they, in turn, would provide her with one or both of these godly resources. The young women can return the scarves and shawls to the ushers as they exit the sanctuary."

Mother Masterson's voice became sharper. "It is our responsibility as the elders of the church to ensure decorum and respectability. It is your job to make it so." Tremors raced through Marnie's body as she recalled zombies in faded suits and matching shoes.

Sister Right concluded, nose high in the air, "We plan to deal with the boys' tattoos, nose rings, multi-colored hair, and gang colors next, but one problem at a time."

Marnie was tired of bullying by people who professed to have a special relationship with God and some keen insight into what God wanted as well as when, why, and how God wanted it! By his own inactivity, Pastor Donaldson tacitly condoned such behavior. Pleased with their suggestion, the women eagerly anticipated Marnie's affirmation and ideas to accomplish their plan. Marnie wanted to give the gaggling group a piece of her mind. She really wanted to tell them that they were probably just plain jealous of young firm bodies, bosoms, and bums! *Not Christ like*, Marnie chided herself. She marshalled the strength to respond with what they needed and not what they deserved. "I cannot tell you how much I appreciate your concern for the spiritual wellbeing of the young people here at Bethlehem. I will be sure to discuss your concerns with Pastor Donaldson and the entire ministerial team during our next meeting. We will consider the pros and cons of your proposal." Marnie believed that people with character were likely to do what they are encouraged to do. Their counterparts are apt to do as they are allowed. And Marnie didn't intend to allow their plan to proceed!

Chapter 12:

Trials by Fire

Could Marnie muster the strength to attend the Governing Board's trainee meeting the next day? Why were they calling a special meeting anyway? She immediately called Clara in hopes of getting more information. Her friend was clueless too. Clara had only heard through Rodney Rollins, who she was dating, about the board's concerns that not all candidates were taking the process seriously. *Clara and Rodney... OMG!* That news actually concerned Marnie more than the unexpected meeting. Who was in trouble? Was it more than one trainee? Probably that lazy legacy Rodney Rollins? *He better not hurt my friend*, Marnie glared.

The rumor was correct. The Governing Board didn't name names, but their concerns reverberated around the room. The candidates eyed one another; they all knew about two or three slack peers. Marnie's stomach dipped. *Were they talking about her? Was she giving it her all? Was God pleased with her progress?* She spent every waking moment that she wasn't working at Bethlehem studying her training manual, reading her notes, and scouring the bible for answers to the myriad theological questions that stumped her. *However, was it enough?*

First Bishop Parker Lowman bellowed, "You are the best of the best, handpicked for this prestigious honor. We didn't pick you." He paused for effect. "God did! God expects you to give your best and to do your best." His wide brow creased.

He handed the microphone to Pastor Maxwell Jepson. "Look at the minister to your left. Now look at the minister to your right. Neither of them will likely meet our high ordination standards." Marnie saw Clara flinch. It might have affected her similarly, but she had heard the same warning during undergraduate orientation. Yet of the three students identified back then, only Marnie had graduated.

Last came Pastor Shelby Lewis. "We won't micromanage you. That would be a great disservice to you. Excellent pastors must be self-motivated. The Holy Spirit should move you toward excellence." She reminded Marnie of Desdemona Stevenson. She peered into each of the candidate's eyes. "You are fearfully and wonderfully made. You will be God's voice, hands, and feet! Just imagine, out of all the people in the world, God believes that each of you can be trusted with God's creation. I believe that too. We all do." Marnie's rapidly beating heart slowed.

The meeting wasn't merely to reprimand idle candidates, but to also remind the diligent ones not to be weary in well-doing for they would surely reap if they didn't faint, commented another board member. Just as some of the trainees gathered their personal belongings to leave, Pastor Lewis said, "Oh, the meeting isn't over. We're just getting started. You have an assignment." Marnie's stomach lurched again. "It's now 7:00 p.m. At 8:00 p.m. each of you should be prepared to provide a fifteen-minute sermon based on a theme randomly drawn from this basket." She raised the receptacle. "Sermons will be timed; exceeding the time allotment automatically constitutes a failing grade. Your sermon must specifically tie the theme to a bible verse, provide practical application, and include a challenge to listeners." Marnie could see tears welling up in Clara's eyes; she lightly rubbed her friend's shaking hands. At least Marnie wasn't the only one scared out of her wits.

Each candidate picked a folded piece of white paper out of the circulating straw basket. Marnie could tell by the look on their face if someone drew a theme they liked or not. Each of them had forty-five minutes to prepare in their assigned room. They could only use their bibles and a writing pad. No laptops or search engines to tempt them. "We want to see what you can do when left to your own ingenuity," challenged Pastor Jepson. To make matters worse, Pastor Donaldson would provide an example sermon first for comparison. *Oh no*, thought Marnie. *He had faults, but no one can out-preach her pastor. They were doomed!*

As she sat at the table in her assigned classroom, Marnie unfolded her selection. She beamed as she read the cursive writing — agape love. *Hallelujah!* Then she flipped open her bible to 2 Timothy 1:1-6 where Paul writes about his love and appreciation for Lois, Eunice, and ultimately, Timothy. She entitled her sermon "Stirred by Love." Words began to fill the notepad. Rather than starting with a definition of *agape* as expected, Marnie began with a

115

personal story about her maternal grandmother, Mamaw. She vividly described her as the glue that bound her family together after her husband died in World War I.

Marnie had listened to Mamaw's stories for hours. She had always found the best in others and had been able to draw the best out of them. It was Mamaw who'd taught Marnie how to bake biscuits and apple pies from scratch. Marnie wrote about how Mamaw had passed down agape or unconditional love, wisdom, commitment to God and family, moxie, and honesty to Marnie's mother — just like the biblical Lois had given her daughter Eunice — and the latter woman had shared with her "dearly beloved son, Timothy." Lastly, Timothy had shared this same love with the Apostle Paul. Marnie challenged listeners to share such love as well because only by doing so would people recognize God's children. Marnie drew parallels between Mamaw and her own mother. She hoped she would be like them one day. She ended by suggesting that Timothy's legacy of unconditional love ran through a line of godly women who had lived out the Great Commandments. Each had inspired the next generation to do the same.

The prep time rushed by and the candidates sat on the front pew as Pastor Donaldson rendered an eloquent, thought-provoking, rousing sermon. He would be a tough act to follow. His sermon included the perfect balance of exegesis, storytelling, humor, and practical knowledge. *However, he's been doing this longer than I've been alive*, thought Marnie. *He has time to prepare a sermon like that because I'm running his church!* She lowered her eyes and avoided eye contact with her pastor. The session turned out to be spiritually uplifting. Smiles and positive vibes warmed the room. Each cleric did well, but Clara was the star of the night.

Clara selected the concept *social justice*. She chose John 10:10-15 as her focal passage. Marnie prayed that Clara's shyness wouldn't derail her sermon. Clara stammered, "My, my sermon title is, 'All About Babe.'" A few trainees chuckled. Clara cleared her voice and raised her head. "This popular movie wasn't just about a pig. It was a universal example of sacrificial leadership and the potential dangers of failing to take responsibility for people in our charge." Her voice became more resolute. "My biblical passage compares Christ, the Good Shepherd, to Satan, the thief." Clara's unexpected take on the passage and imagery drew every listener into her exegetical world. "Many people come to church looking for safety and protection from the thief in order to deal with social injustices like poverty, sexism, racism, and other problems created and perpetuated by the thief. If we wish to be Good Shepherds, we must fight the negative experiences we are bound to have at the hands of church folks and focus on their potential as Christians — and all the more on the unsaved." Marnie nodded. "Yes, yes." Clara's voice became increasingly sure with every syllable.

"If there is any Christ in us at all, how can we ignore the cries of the dejected and brokenhearted? Just as the unexpected little pig, Babe, became his group's leader, the tiny babe in the manger, Christ, grew up to become the Savior of the world. Although the former is no comparison to the perfection and majesty of the latter, like the tiny pig in the famous, funny film, we can become more than others than we ever imagine when we put the lives and liberties of other people before our own." She lifted her arms skyward. "We too can be like Christ and become present-day Good Shepherds." Clara then pointed directly toward the audience with her right finger. "But like Him, we *must* be willing to sacrifice our very lives for humanity." No one would ever question whether the shy woman was trainee material. With one sermon, Clara became the top contender. She stood fixed for a moment before receiving a standing ovation. Even Rodney brushed away tears. Later that night, Marnie sobbed as Clara's words resounded in her ears.

Chapter 13:

Nuns and Safe Spaces

Monica and Marnie met for a late lunch at their favorite restaurant Popp's Porch, known for its eclectic, organic fusion fare. Moreover, its bohemian clientele almost ensured that they wouldn't run into a *church* crowd. The two female clerics discovered a place where they could just breathe. After sharing pecan encrusted salmon with sautéed asparagus and the restaurant's famous pouli roti and maple bacon-infused waffles, they window shopped at nearby boutiques. "Time for dessert. My treat!" shouted Monica. They giggled like schoolgirls as chocolate chunk frozen custard gave them brain freezes. After catching a last-minute movie, they ended up on the back deck of Marnie's condominium just in time to sip warm lemon tea and watch the sunset. A common day made uncommon by their chaotic schedules.

"How long has it been?" Marnie spoke in her best friend's direction but gazed at the sun slipping away.

"Too long... probably a few months for sure. That's a problem. We promised to do this at least once a month," said Monica. "Times just seems to get away from us."

"I just can't seem to get in front of this time thing. So many things to do, so little time. However, my responsibilities pale in comparison to yours. I'm not a pastor," Marnie acknowledged.

"Not yet." Monica raised her cup of tea in a toast. "Here's to pending ordinations and future pastorates."

"Thanks, but sometimes I wonder whether I even want those responsibilities. I watch you, Monica. You are my litmus test for pastoral ministry. I see what you do. The things and people you contend with and the way you balance multiple, sometimes conflicting hats. I can't imagine all the work that I *don't* see."

"Don't you mean *juggle* many hats?" Monica was talented and self-effacing — and loved for it by Marnie, friends, and congregants alike. Marnie fidgeted and crossed her legs several times. "Stop worrying, girl. You're ready for ordination. Moreover, you will be ready to pastor when the time comes. God will make sure you get the right church at exactly the right time." Monica squinted toward the fast escaping sun.

"That's what Dad said too. You both have more confidence in me than I seem to have in myself. I guess this ordination thing means so much to me. I'm stressing myself out. I know, scripture says not to be worried about anything. I'm working on that," Marnie confessed through a slight grin. "I know it might sound crazy, but this entire ordination process is one of the best times I've ever had! I love what I am learning and the challenge. Love the discussions with the other candidates. I even like the assignments." Monica didn't comment as her friend began to rub her elbows. "I'm serious. Really! However, I'm scared as heck of failing. I want to make sure I'm the best minister I can be."

"I know, Marn. Very Type A. Remember, no matter how much you study and learn you won't be perfect. None of us are," Monica said.

"I know that. I know I'm not perfect. I'm talking about being excellent for God. Knowing that I'm giving my best," Marnie retorted.

"Just reminding, not criticizing. So that you won't be so hard on yourself. Which is something you tend to do." Monica grinned, leaning her head slightly to the right the way she did when giving advice. Although they were the same age, Monica completed ordination five years prior and with flying colors while Marnie was completing her PhD in religious studies. A terminal degree at a prestigious university sealed Marnie's academic fate. She wanted to make sure that if she ever hit a glass ceiling, it wouldn't be because of the lack of education. However, it would take more than credentials to be a great minister. By watching her father and Monica, Marnie knew that the role of servant required a heart for people with all their problems and promise. *Do I have that kind of heart for the people after what happened to Big Ed?*

Despite vacillating emotions, Marnie always knew that she was called to preach. She remembered her seven-year-old self perched on the family love seat watching her favorite movie, *The Song of Bernadette*. The film had documented the ninteenth century peasant girl's unfailing faith in God, unconditional love of people, selflessness, peaceful spirit, and steadfast service in the face of physical travail. *That's what I want to be when I grow up!*

After fumbling through a well-worn encyclopedia, Marnie had scampered off to find her mother. "Mom! Mom!" She had been sure she'd burst if she didn't share the news. "Mom, I want to be a nun!" Mrs. Hunter had been drying the last dinner plate. Marnie had bounced back and forth on her feet; her mother had not responded.

"Mom? Did you hear me? I said want to be a nun like Bernadette Soubirous! I read that she even became a saint!" Mrs. Hunter had folded the washcloth and gingerly hung it on the rack below the sink. Still no response. "Didn't you hear me?" The little girl had scratched her head.

"Honey," her mother had paused, leaned down, and caressed Marnie's right cheek. "Sweetie, you can't become a nun." She had kissed her forehead. Marnie's brow had ruffled.

"What do you mean I can't become a nun? I can do whatever I want to do. It's my life. I can become whatever I want to. You can't stop me. No one can stop me. God is on my side!" A mass of muddled words and sounds had shot from Marnie's mouth, her tiny arms had thrashed, and flicks of perspiration had begun to bead on her forehead. In one swoop, Mrs. Hunter had picked up and swaddled her daughter in her lap on a kitchen chair.

"Honey, you didn't let me finish. You can be absolutely anything you want to be. I'm excited to see what you become." Marnie had gazed up into her mother's warm green eyes. She had gradually unfolded her little fists. "What I mean is you can't become a nun at this time, because you aren't Catholic." Marnie's first theological lesson on faith traditions had occurred cradled in her mother's arms. About an hour later,

Mrs. Hunter had lightly pecked Marnie's nose. "Does that make sense to you, Marn? Now if you decide that you want to become Catholic, your father and I will gladly help you. However, if you still want to be part of our denomination, Christian Community, that's fine too. God is God."

"I'll stick with CC for the time being," Marnie had yawned and rubbed her eyes as Mrs. Hunter had carried her to bed. Even back then Marnie had gotten the profession right, the role was just different. Monica's voice pulled Marnie back into the present.

"You've known you've been called — forever. This ordination thing is just a blip on the radar of what will be a lifetime of service. We don't need their approval. It's just a nice rite of passage, especially for women." Monica's head tilted to the right again. "You've got what it takes to be a great pastor or anything else you want to be. I've always admired the impassioned, practical way you see things. And you're ethical to a fault. You've always known that everyone is important, but everyone's opinion isn't. Moreover, you are able to balance that truth. Believe me, it's easier said than done." Monica paused as if preparing to rip a Band-Aid off a flinching child. "Sometimes you're your worst enemy. I don't know where in the world your standard comes from. I love you for it, but damn, sometimes it's just too much. Sometimes it's unrealistic. Give yourself a break, why don't you!" She suddenly stuck out her tongue. Marnie grinned.

"I'm not finished yet. Here's something else to think about. You can keep things pretty close to the vest. You have a wonderful knack for helping other people open up and you *think* you're open, but you keep so much bottled up. It scares me sometimes." Monica snatched off the last bandage.

"Remember when you came back from that accident in the country about five years ago? Scratches covered your face and legs. Bandages wrapped your arms. It took months before you could even drive again. Nevertheless, you told us, 'Oh, I was in an accident.' That's all. You looked like hell warmed over, but all we got out of you was, 'Oh, I was in an accident.' We didn't press you, but we've always wondered. Still do. I know you. I believe that you will tell us the truth when you are ready." Marnie looked out the bay window into the blackness. The two friends sipped tea in silence. An hour later, they hugged goodbye.

The following day, the candidates held their final group training session before oral exams. This last session would be a theological discussion. *Not another theological discussion*, Marnie grimaced. *I've been having these discussions since I was seven years old.* Pastor Jepson called the group to order. "We'll divide you into two teams. The assignment covers two controversial biblical passages. After you get a passage, each team can confer for thirty minutes. Then you should provide a coherent introduction followed by rebuttals. The debate will continue for thirty minutes. We will determine which team provides the more thoughtful responses. You're working in teams, but each of you will also be evaluated based on your individual contributions."

Bishop Lowman peered over his black-framed spectacles. "Looking forward to the results."

Despite the pending test, Marnie felt unusually giddy. She had talked with Jeremy the night before! "I've missed you," She cooed.

"I've missed you more," Jeremy had purred using his sexy librarian voice. They had picked up right where they had left off. Memories of that horrid fight had evaporated like mist.

"Congratulations on your progress toward ordination. I knew you would knock it out," he had said.

"Thanks, babe. I'm so proud of your promotion and raise at the library." They had giggled and joked like school children and had even had a little phone sex to boot! "I'll meet you later today at your place. Rose in hand. I'll bring dinner. You're the dessert." Marnie hoped no one saw her blush. But now Marnie needed to focus on the task at hand.

"The parallel passages for discussion are **Matthew 26:13-15, Mark 14:9-11, and Luke 22:2-4,**" commanded Bishop Lowman. "Please convene to your respective classrooms. Again, you have thirty minutes." The candidates scurried to maximize their time. *Clara's on my team. Yes!* Marnie beamed. Hosea, Joe Lewis, and Constance were great additions too. The second team included Rodney, Frank, Janie, Bonita, and Keith. They had to debate about the nature of sin and whether certain sins are unforgivable. Judas Iscariot in the life of Jesus Christ would be key.

Both teams started strong as confirmed by the nodding heads of the Governing Board. Rodney made the next statement on behalf of his team. "It is our contention that Judas Iscariot's biblical role was pre-ordained and crucial. Although he is known across history as an antagonist, his actions set in motion the needed *devilment*, for lack of a better word, from which Christ would save the world." Despite his unorthodox vocabulary, his team supported his viewpoint. Marnie's team responded.

"We agree, in part, with Rodney's thought processes," stated Marnie, the designated speaker. "We question most biblical interpretations that consider Judas some sort of automaton destined to betray Christ. Like each of us, he had free will. Although Christ knew that Judas would betray him, Iscariot could have still chosen a different path. We make the distinction between God's perfect will and God's permissive will. Under the former state, sin wouldn't even exist. Therefore, Judas would have chosen another path. In fact, there would have been no need for Christ to come to earth as He did." She hoped her remarks didn't seem tautological. "However, because of God's permissive will, like Adam and Eve, Judas had options. Yet once he made that fateful choice to betray Christ, he forced humanity down a path that would require redemption." Her group affirmed Marnie's response.

Rodney hastily replied and without conferring with his team. "Although we agree with your definitions of perfect and permissive will, we believe the response is a bit shortsighted. In *my* estimation, I'm sorry, in *our* estimation, Judas couldn't have chosen to betray Christ without some skewed internal barometer… some terrible character flaw." His team's eyes darted in Rodney's direction. Board members jotted notes, eyes downturned.

After conferring with her team, Marnie simply said, "We disagree that Judas' nature was somehow different from those of the other eleven." Joe Lewis completed the argument.

"Just as James, John, Peter and certainly each disciple was imperfect, so was Judas. Yet his propensity to sin was no different from theirs. Even good people, Christians, make mistakes. Although the consequences of those mistakes may vary dramatically." The team members nodded in support. Marnie couldn't have provided a better retort. Moreover, *she had to believe it.* If it weren't true, her experience with Big Ed had surely sealed her fate!

The teams verbally volleyed several more rounds, refining their respective theological arguments. With each round, a member of the board commented, challenged flawed arguments, and corrected errors. The opposing team made their final comment. To Marnie, they sidestepped the centrality of the Gospel message of free will. They also seemed unable to reconcile the biblically-based belief that no matter how egregious in their outcomes or consequences, all sins can be forgiven.

Pastor Lewis announced the results. "The goal wasn't to select a winner or loser, but rather to provide insight. Both teams did a great job." Yet the outcome favored Marnie's team. As she strutted toward her car, Pastor Jepson mumbled in her direction. "Good job, Minister Hunter." Later that night Marnie mulled over the debate. The bible was clear that sins could be forgiven. It was equally clear about the need to reconcile with your neighbor. Marnie had some unfinished business. As she reflected, Marnie realized that, in some ways, she was stuck on the side of that country road watching silently while being consumed in flames. She would have to go back and reconcile her past if she ever hoped to be whole again or to have a future as one of God's servants.

Chapter 14:

Toiling in the Shadows

Much to the dismay of the MOB, a critical mass of younger women at Bethlehem thought the church was too "otherworldly" at the expense of real-world issues. "We focus too much on going to heaven and ignore people who are living like hell," the president of the Young Adult Ministry complained. They wanted something more. They just didn't know what.

Pastor Donaldson announced during their weekly one-on-one meeting, "Minister Hunter, after much prayer, I'd like you to take leadership of this new women's initiative. I know you can make it happen! As the lead female minister, it is only fitting that you take the helm. I think it needs a *woman's touch.*"

Marnie fumed, but took notes as Pastor Donaldson passed the responsibility for yet another major church event off to her. *What a dweeb!* To assume that somehow men and women can't plan events for each other. They've been doing it for ages. She believed that both groups at Bethlehem could benefit from working together. Marnie lowered her eyes and kept her mouth shut.

"Because your plate is already full," he affirmed in passing. "Mothers Masterson and Peters and Sister Right have volunteered to help you. I know they can be prickly sometimes, but they have valuable institutional history. Please try to work with them." *I'm not the problem.* The women would meet the following Sunday.

Well over one hundred women, young and old, and several girls attended the inaugural planning meeting. Their beaming faces mirrored her own as Marnie stood behind the podium. The MOB sauntered down the sanctuary aisle late. Mothers Masterson and Peters, and Sister Right sat shoulder to shoulder on the front pew; their subordinates scattered throughout the other women. Marnie felt sweat bead on her back. After an opening prayer, she said, "Women and young ladies of Bethlehem, thank you so much for attending our first meeting as we expand our women's ministry. God has given us a chance to do something new in the history of this great church! We are so very blessed." Marnie really believed those words. Now if she could only convince them.

She distributed an agenda that included the church calendar of their standing events for the year. "We can decide if we want these existing events to continue, revise them to emphasize new issues, or substitute others. Any thoughts?" Marnie methodically moved down the agenda. A variety of women, including a few younger girls, raised their hands with questions and provided creative input, comments, and critiques. Everyone agreed that certain mainstay events should continue, but they wanted more events that focus on women's issues, women in the Bible, and practical topics they could select. Marnie's sense of satisfaction was short-lived. Mother Masterson, who grimaced from the start, interrupted the assembly.

"Excuse me, Minister Hunter." Marnie could practically taste the saccharin in her words. "I am so excited about our plans! If done correctly, this will be a wonderful opportunity for the young women to learn from us seasoned saints." *Seasoned is right — with vinegar.* Some of the younger women rolled their eyes before looking in Marnie's direction. Several younger girls started to squirm. Mother Masterson extended the thin, withered pointer finger on her right hand directly at Marnie.

"I would like to make several points. Although events like cooking and exercise classes might be fun, I don't quite understand how they are godly or how they reflect a biblical emphasis on how to be Christian women. Secondly, I think it only appropriate that the older women, particularly the mother's group, be responsible for leading and organizing the bulk of the events. Moreover, I have spoken to Pastor Donaldson about our concerns. I thought he would be here today to make sure that everything is done decently and in order." Salt and pepper heads bobbed on the front row and throughout the group. Yet Marnie could tell that the majority didn't agree. "Furthermore, we must address serious malfeasances such as inappropriate clothing, hairstyles, jewelry, and the like," Mother Matheson sneered. *Here we go again.*

One of the younger women with a purple buzz cut replied. "Hairstyles? Hair? Are you serious? If you are so concerned about hair, the next time I cut mine, I will put it in a bag and give it to you." *Touché.*

Sister Right turned and glared at the young woman. "Many of you just don't know any better. We're here to teach you." *Lord, Lord. These old biddies are crazy.* Marnie dug the tip of her ink pen deep into her notepad.

"The bible says that young people should be seen and not heard," spat Sister Right.

"Actually, Sister Right that is an old English proverb. No matter. At Bethlehem, we want everyone to be heard." Marnie didn't even look in the elderly woman's direction. "I'm sure Pastor Donaldson would agree with me." Her brow wrinkled.

"See, I told you guys." The president of the Young Adult Ministry looked around at her group members. "Nobody wants to listen to us." She threw up her hands.

Mother Masterson ignored the young woman's remark. "Minister Hunter, you don't know our ways here at Bethlehem. We have a rich tradition that absolutely must be maintained." Marnie had a flashback of the Chet Cargill catastrophe. *Enough is enough.*

"Everyone, let's just stop and breathe for a few moments." Marnie audibly pushed air out of her lungs and lowered her arms to her sides, palms facing forward. "Many of you voiced your opinions. God bless you and thank you. Please know that I am listening." Her lips curled in a brief smile aimed at the Young Adult Ministry leader. "It's my responsibility to shepherd this process. I know we can work together to do something that will please God and meet our holistic needs." She stepped away from the podium and stood directly in the middle of the entire group, forcing the MOB to strain their necks backwards to see her. "Please let me finish presenting what I believe to be a multifaceted schedule." "Amen. Amen," anonymously rose from the crowd. "We want to feed our spirits, fellowship together, eat good food, and have some fun!" Marnie exclaimed.

"Amen, Rev. Hunter," agreed several more attendees.

"Remember, this is a proposed scheduled. I'm open for other activities. Although I am the designated Chair, this will definitely be a collaborative effort!"

"I'm concerned about having youth on committees," chimed Sister Peters. "What do they know about organizing and leading?" She frowned in Marnie's direction.

"Well, Sister Peters, that's the very reason they need to be involved." Marnie paused a moment. "Additionally, to address the comment about Bethlehem's traditions and my place in them. Many of you know that I spent some time at this church. My father was pastor here for over five years. I am well aware of Bethlehem's rich traditions. My family and I are part of them. Moreover, it's true, I am relatively new here… as a minister. I've been here fewer than two years. I am proud of that fact because we need to combine the best of Bethlehem's traditions with some new blood." Amens drowned out MOB mumbles. Two older women stomped out of the meeting, but Mother Masterson remained glued to the pew.

Marnie continued unflustered. "2 Timothy 1:7 reminds us that 'God has not given us the spirit of fear, but of power, love, and a sound mind.' Please remember that verse. There is no precedent here, so the sky is the limit. As this verse reminds us, let's not be afraid to try new things. Ministry can take many exciting forms. Let's be empowered to make thoughtful decisions moving forward. Most importantly, whatever we do and say, let it come from a place of love." The women stood and applauded. Mother Masterson clapped begrudgingly but remained affixed to her seat. After moving through the remainder of the agenda and scheduling the next meeting, Marnie asked a teenager to give a closing prayer. As she collected her papers, bible, and bags, women continued to stroll by, shake her hand, and nod.

After finally arriving at home, Marnie slumped onto her couch. Had she been holding her breath that entire meeting? Some progress, some pitfalls. She realized that she would have to lead by example. Practice what she preached. She could faintly hear Dr. Irene Calgary's voice. "Wrong attitude, no gratitude, and no latitude." This meant she would have to stop referring to the elderly women of the church, no matter how challenging they might be, as MOBs. That would be the first step in the right direction.

Chapter 15:

Marnie Take the Wheel

Thirty-two youth met Marnie in the Family Life Center just as the sun peeked through the clouds. She and three other women would serve as chaperones for their annual day trip to Fun Land, an amusement park in the neighboring city. Most of the youth were under the age of 13 years old; all of them hailed from Bethlehem Church. The younger kids laughed and chatted in anticipation of scurrying from ride to ride and tasting carnival treats. Despite cool poses and smartphones tethered to their hands, even the teens always enjoyed riding the park's seven roller coasters and sampling their way through food kiosks. Most of their parents would only allow them to attend the trip if Marnie was lead chaperone. Neither Pastor Donaldson nor the bus driver had arrived. Everyone was snacking on Krisy Kreme donuts, sipping orange juice, and waiting.

The young people had been anticipating the trip for months. Most had busted their humps to raise money for their tickets by washing cars and selling cookies and cupcakes at church bake sales. Marnie surveyed the group with pride and tried to squash her usual fears of being responsible for anyone under four feet tall. However, she hadn't visited an amusement park since she was a teenager, so she secretly looked forward to Fun Land. As she took a final sip of juice, her cell phone rang. Marnie heard Pastor Donaldson's voice on the other end; her heart sank.

"Minister Hunter, thank God I reached you. I have some bad news. I won't be able to come with the team to Fun Land. Something has come up that I must address so I will meet you there later today. Lunch is on me. I know you can handle everything there. Just be the excellent leader that you are!" Marnie could sense his smile through the telephone. She wasn't smiling. She hated his perkiness and she hated the fact that she hated it! An image of a Shadow Pastor emerged in Marnie's thoughts. *Duped again, but it's for the kids. Do it for the kids,* She reminded herself.

"That's fine, Pastor. I understand. We're waiting for a few children. However, the bus driver is not here."

"Mr. Parker's not there yet? That's surprising. He's always early. Let me call and light a fire under him," joked Pastor Donaldson.

"Thanks, Pastor. I'll be waiting for your call back. If he gets here before then, I'll let you know," she replied.

Marnie and the other chaperones were counting heads, assigning partners, checking lunches, and collecting permission slips as the final few youth strolled through the door. The younger kids were beginning to play tag around rows of chairs, crawl on the floor, and dash along the front stage. The older ones sat in quiet corners wearing ear buds with their heads leaned against the walls. Mr. Parker still hadn't arrived. Marnie hoped that he was all right. Her cell phone rang again and her heart dipped a second time.

"Reverend Hunter, I'm so sorry, but I have some terrible news!" It was a noticeably less perky Pastor Donaldson. "Mr. Parker has the stomach flu. He's sick as a dog." Marnie groused. "He can't drive the bus. I've been trying to get another driver, but no such luck. We will have to cancel the trip." Disappointment dripped from his voice.

She stood up and walked out of earshot of the antsy group. "Pastor, we can't cancel the trip. The kids have looked forward to it all year. You know how hard they've worked to raise money. They'll be heartbroken."

"I know, Minister Hunter. I don't know what to do. At this juncture, we just don't have a driver." She knew he was all for gender parity. However, she also knew he was probably concerned about a busload of kids and female chaperones without an adult male in the bunch. Marnie's sexism radar was at the ready, but she had to admit her own concerns.

"I understand, Pastor. Mr. Parker is a seasoned bus driver and a mechanic. That bus has seen better days."

"I really hate to ask, but how do you feel about driving the bus there? I know you have your license to drive large vehicles. If you don't drive, we'll have to cancel."

"Yes, I have my chauffeur's license, but I don't know…"

"Minister Hunter, I *promise* to get on the road as soon as I can and meet you there. I will drive the bus back and you can drive my car. So all you have to do is get them there. What do you say?" *It's for the kids. Do it for the kids.*

Although Bethlehem's church colors, name, and insignia were emblazoned on both of its sides, it was still a rickety, old school bus. No air condition, no seatbelts, no restroom. Marnie's mouth fell open as she eyed the heap. *The only things keeping this bucket of bolts together are rust and prayer.* She prayed that it would at least last for their trip. The young people didn't care who was driving. They jockeyed for seats. However, several chaperones look surprisingly in Marnie's direction. After a final roll call and a prayer for safe travels, Marnie got behind the wheel. She hoped no one noticed how far she adjusted the driver's seat forward so her feet would reach the pedals. Her right hand shook as she turned the ignition and swallowed hard. *No turning back now.* She could do this. She was trained to do this. She met all the requirements to do it. So all Marnie had to do was do it.

She turned right out of the church parking lot and headed toward the interstate. It was a Saturday morning, so the roads were busier than usual. Yet the five hundred pounds of burgundy parted cars like the Red Sea. Marnie stayed in the rightmost lane and kept the speed limit. The children never seemed to exhaust their inventory of songs — *He's Got the Whole World in His Hands*; *Jesus Loves the Little Children*; *Yes, Jesus Loves Me*; and *B-I--N-G-O*. The adults giggled as the youth mangled a medley of church, popular, rock & roll and R&B songs. None of them were choir members, several were clearly tone-deaf, but their renditions were infectious.

Banter grew each time they spotted another billboard about the distance to Fun Land. The miles flew by. About thirty miles from their destination, several thundering booms interrupted a second stanza of B-I-N-G-O. The bus violently lurched to the right amidst screeching sounds and high-pitched screams. Marnie instinctively turned the steering wheel to the left to prevent the bus from veering off the highway. The chaperones couldn't quiet the children's escalating screams and sobs; teens pulled out their ear buds and eyeballed the reeling bus.

Marnie realized that at least one tire on the right side of the bus was blown. She flicked on the flashers and began the careful work to keep the bus from tipping over. "Everyone, stay calm. Everything is under control." Maybe she could convince herself. The other women echoed her promise to the young passengers. Marnie could hear the steel rim screeching as it dragged along the asphalt. Rather than slam on the brakes and risk losing control, she tapped the lever with her right foot to slow the sluggish vehicle. "Please children. Stay calm. Everything will be all right. Listen to Sisters Rucker, Poppy, and Burns."

Then Marnie smelled smoke and flashed back to that dark rural road. Smoke meant fire and fire meant death. *Be calm. Stay cool.* She needed to stop the bus fast, but an abrupt stop might cause it to careen and flip over. "Sister Rucker, please make sure the children are all seated." Marnie called out behind her above the piercing screams. There were no seat belts, so nothing could keep the young riders secured. *Help us, God!* Marnie was responsible for thirty-five souls. She had lost someone thrusted into her care before, she wouldn't lose anyone else. She called out again. "Everyone, hold on to the back of the seat in front of you. Sisters Rucker, Poppy, and Burns, help them." Bodies jostled and jolted as the screams continued and smoke spread.

God has not given us the spirit of fear, but of power, love, and a sound mind. Her favorite bible verse became a Balm in Gilead. Power. Love. Sound mind. God's promises to the faithful. Then a sense of peace replaced the images of fiery vehicles, burning flesh, and smoke-filled spaces. Marnie continued to tap the brake rhythmically. She could feel the vehicle slowing. However, it continued to lurch right and left. Bodies followed. Each time it lurched, Marnie countered gingerly in the opposite direction. *Keep it balanced, Marnie. Drive the bus decently and in order.* Although the staggering motions continued, the bus didn't topple. After several minutes that felt like hours, Marnie slowed the screeching, smoking bus, maneuvered it off the highway, and pulled the emergency brake.

The smell of smoke and fumes hung in the air. "Everybody off the bus. Single file! Now!" She then saw the damage. Sister Rucker cradled her bloody head several rows back. Marnie could hear Tommy Thompson's continued shrieks. "Sister Poppy, please lead the children out and move as far from the highway as you can get. Sister Burns, please help Sister Rucker. Wrap this around her head." Marnie handed her the abandoned jacket in arm's reach. I'll help Tommy." She rushed past youth moving in the opposite direction until she got to the seat where Tommy was looking down at his right arm. "Tommy, honey. I'm going to pick you up. I know it hurts, but we've got to get off the bus. Okay?" He nodded.

Marnie cradled his shivering body off the bus. By then he was only whimpering. Soon the entire group was standing or sitting in a grassy cut a safe distance from both traffic and the smoking bus. Sister Rucker was moving in and out of consciousness and Tommy began crying again. *God, please let them be all right!* Marnie silently repeated this prayer relentlessly.

Sister Poppy had already called 911 and several police cars soon pulled up behind the metal frame still tipped precariously to the right. Tiny gray smoke circles continued to escape from beneath the bus as officers placed emergency cones on the scene. Marnie continued to hold Tommy while Sister Poppy moved through the group of traumatized children, distributing hugs and kisses. Marnie looked over a sea of scrapes, cuts, and bruises. She used her jacket to clean tiny blood trails from Tommy's head while caressing his tasseled hair.

Two EMT vehicles drove up behind the police cars. One medic placed a splint on Tommy's arm; another placed a neck brace on a dazed Sister Rucker. Marnie mouthed "thank you" toward the injured chaperone and kissed Tommy's chubby cheek. The same vehicle whisked the two away. The two remaining medics patiently checked each passenger and applied peroxide and bandages as needed. "The kids seem okay. Just a little rattled. You should still take them to the hospital for a thorough examination. Possible internal damages would be hard to detect out here. Their parents might want to observe them over the next few weeks for emotional trauma that might surface."

Marnie thanked both the police and the EMTs and updated her group. "Tommy and Sister Rucker are going to be fine. No worries. We all must go to the hospital for an examination. I promise that we will reschedule the trip later this month. You all have been so very brave. I'm so proud of you." Sister Poppy mentioned that Pastor Donaldson was on his way.

The first police officer at the scene retraced his steps back to Marnie. "Ma'am, I just have a few more questions and several forms for you to sign." He was especially kind as he surveyed the now chattering young brood. "Based on the scene, no one seems to be at fault here. The two back tires on the right side of the bus simply blew out. I want to commend you, ma'am, for keeping a calm head. It was good that you quickly got that bus off the highway to avoid other vehicles. You were lucky. You saved a busload of people from serious injury or worse."

"Thank you, Officer." Marnie knew that luck had nothing to do with it. She gave another silent prayer of thanks. The same officer vowed to stay until the repair crew arrived. Several minutes later, the roadside assistance truck replaced the two useless tires. The repairperson confirmed that the smoke was the result of the metal parts of the bus, both tire and bus frame, meeting asphalt.

As the repair crew completed its final tasks, Pastor Donaldson drove up and stopped behind the line of service vehicles. He shook the officer's hand while moving towards his littlest members. "Thank God you're all right. I love each of you!" He began to share hugs, pat heads, and joke with a few teenagers. Some of the children complained of being hungry. "We must get you checked out by doctors before you eat anything. Guess what. I heard you were supposed to go to Burger Heaven after the trip. So next weekend, we'll meet at the church and Burger Heaven's on me!" The youngsters cheered at the thought of free heavenly burgers, fries, and shakes.

Several doe-eyed youngsters said in unison, "Miss Marnie said we were coming back to Fun Land next month. Can we?"

"Well, if Miss Marnie said it, then it is sure to happen." Marnie was standing within earshot of the conversation. The pastor gave her a hug that lasted longer than she expected. "Oh, Marnie." His lower lip quivered. "Oh, Marnie. Thank you." Formalities were lost in the day's events. "I am so sorry this happened. I am sorrier that I wasn't here. Thank God, everyone is all right. I'm going to see Sister Rucker and Tommy later tonight. I notified the church secretary and she is calling all the parents. I'll call Tommy's mother and Brother Rucker myself. We don't want to alarm anyone. It's better that we update them rather than the evening news." Diplomacy meant Marnie would delay addressing the situation.

"Yes Pastor, everything is okay. We are fortunate. Most of the children seem okay, just a bit shaken. We were just about to leave for the emergency room. Better safe than sorry."

He repeated, "I am so glad you were here. If something like this had to happen, thank God you were in charge." *Had to happen!* Ire simmered in her stomach. However, she squelched the comment aching to spew from her mouth. She believed that his genuine concern was getting lost in theology and thoughts about lawsuits. Marnie wasn't in the mood.

"Pastor," she said, "the other chaperones and children were such quick thinkers. We helped each other make the best out of what could have been a very terrible situation." She didn't want to make him feel guilty, but she didn't mind if he squirmed a little. "God was looking out for us." She turned and strode back toward the roadside team.

"Well ma'am, we've got the tires all fixed. You're good as new." The roadside mechanic beamed in Marnie's direction. "Please sign here." Although Pastor Donaldson was standing beside Marnie, he didn't try to take the lead. "Several of the other tires seem a bit old. You maybe should check and replace them. Not trying to tell you what to do, but the church should probably think about getting a new bus, especially if you're transporting kids." His voice slowed. "Those new charter vans are top-of-the-line. They've got seatbelts, multiple escape doors, bathrooms — the works." Marnie nodded at the well-meaning man, signed the invoice, and shook his hand as he gave her a copy of the receipt. After thanking the lead police officer one final time, everyone mounted the bus. The officer again promised to follow them several miles to road test the repairs.

Pastor Donaldson pulled Marnie aside, but avoided eye contact. "Do you feel up to driving the bus back? I can do it… if you want. You can drive my car."

"Thanks, Pastor Donaldson, but I like to finish what I start." He didn't press the issue, but asked Sister Poppy to drive his car so that he could ride on the bus. After everyone found a seat, he gave a prayer of thanksgiving and for safe journey that seemed longer than usual. The bus left the potentially tragic scene in its wake.

Most of the parents anxiously met them at the hospital. Several hours later, each child received a clean bill of health and snacks for their growling, empty stomachs. Most of the children left with their parents, but not before parents and children thanked Marnie and the two remaining chaperones. By about 9:00 p.m., Sisters Poppy and Burns, Pastor Donaldson, and eight remaining children trudged off the bus into the cool night air of the church parking lot. A few moments later, this final escort of youth was on its way home with their respective parents.

The challenges of the day were finally beginning to take their toll on the young minister. "You both are angels. I'll never forget it." Marnie hugged the two chaperones and watched them get into their vehicles. Each promised to chaperone the rescheduled trip. She had a newfound respect for members of Bethlehem. Despite busy schedules, jobs, and their own problems and needs, most of them served the church and community as volunteers. Marnie slowly plodded toward her car, rubbing the back of her neck and elbows. She gave one final wave as their cars disappeared into the night. Only she and Pastor Donaldson now stood in the empty parking lot.

"Marnie, I know tomorrow's Sunday, but why don't you take the day off. One of the other ministers can officiate." Based on the day's events, Pastor Donald Donaldson was extending an olive branch.

"Thanks a lot, Pastor, but a lot is happening tomorrow. None of the other ministers know exactly what to do. I should be here to make sure things run smoothly. I'll be all right after a good night's rest. Take care. See you tomorrow morning." Sapped, she just couldn't verbally dance with him. Fully addressing the day's events would require more time and energy than she could muster. However, things would have to be addressed — and soon.

Several hours later, the steaming bath water engulfed the young cleric's frame. It was much hotter than she usually liked, but Marnie knew that the heat, combined with heaps of Epson salt she added, would ferret out the aches and pains from her tired, sore body and mind. The glass of red wine beckoning from the tub's edge would help too. Later, as she lay in bed, the phone buzzed. She already updated the Seminary Sisters about the day's excitement via text. They responded with animated emojis. Each friend was also livid at Pastor Donaldson, conveyed by lines of angry-faced emojis. Marnie chuckled, but was too exhausted to respond further. After promising to see them at their next get-together the following week, Marnie was just about to doze off when she noticed Jeremy's name on the caller ID. She texted him while they were standing on the roadside but convinced him not to drive there. Jeremy would've been great help, but Marnie was afraid he might deck Pastor Donaldson — and that she wouldn't stop him! *Let's delay that talk as long as possible.* She did pick up her dad's call.

After a noticeably long pause, he said, "Hi, Marn. How are you feeling?" His voice was thick with skepticism. *Maybe I should've delayed this talk as well.* It was too late for that. Maybe this talk was a long time coming.

"I'm fine, Dad. Just a little achy."

"Your mom is sitting right here. She will be relieved to know that you are okay." Marnie heard him exhale. "You had a busy day." His voice trailed off.

"Yep. It was unexpected and unusual. You've always said that a good minister is always prepared. You know, one sermon in your bible, one in your pocket, and one in your head." A feigned giggle was stuck in her throat.

"That's true, Marn, but you're taking my words a bit out of context."

"I know, Dad. I know that you're probably mad at what I got myself into today. Everything turned out... fine."

"Listen, Marn. I know it's late and you're probably bushed. Moreover, knowing you as I do, you are still planning to attend church tomorrow. I won't hold you, but we *will* have a conversation about this. Can your mother and I expect you for dinner tomorrow as usual? She's making your favorites — pecan encrusted salmon, asparagus, twice-backed sweet potatoes, and her homemade wheat rolls." Despite any reservations about their pending conversation, he knew that this menu would ensure Marnie's presence at dinner.

"I wouldn't miss it. Love you, Dad. Tell Mom the same. Night." Marnie expected to be read the Riot Act the next day, but she looked forward to their safe harbor.

Chapter 16:

Guess Who's Coming to

Communion?

Despite the bus accident, Marnie felt surprisingly energized the following Sunday and glided through each service. Mishaps were minimal and actually took her mind off other looming church matters. Pastor Donaldson's sermons were unusually motivational. Although she heard it said many times, Marnie now knew how potentially life-threatening experiences could make you appreciate the important things in life. She didn't know how she would address the bus incident, but she was relieved that the injuries were few. News about what would go down in Bethlehem history as the *Fun Land Fiasco* spread like wildfire. Services were thick with hugs, handshakes, kisses, and thank yous from adults and youth alike. No one wanted to imagine life without Bethlehem's children.

"I received news this morning that Sister Rucker will be released from Mt. Sinai late next week. She hit her head pretty hard, so the doctors want to continue to monitor her concussion. Be sure to pray for her and, if you have time, I'm sure she'd enjoy a visit. Little Tommy Thompson is running around here somewhere showing off his arm cast. Be sure to sign it! Much thanks Minister Hunter and Sisters Rucker, Poppy, and Burns for their *selflessness and sheroism*." Pastor Donaldson paused and his bottom lip trembled. "Their quick thinking helped avoid a potentially devastating accident. Bethlehem is very blessed." The congregation gave the chaperones a standing ovation during both worship services. "We are retiring that old bus and purchasing a brand new coach. Only the best for Bethlehem." More applause. After Marnie officiated over Communion, each chaperone received a certificate of appreciation in a silver-embossed frame. Jeremy winked at her from his usual spot in the pews. *Maybe he's not mad anymore,* she hoped.

Marnie was actually a bit uncomfortable with all the attention that day. After church, Tommy Thompson dashed by, only breaking long enough for Marnie to scribble her name on his armored limb. Did he resemble Lil' Ed? Picking up stray hymnals at the end of the final service, she turned a corner right into the outstretched, time-creased arms of Mother Masterson. "Oh, Rev. Hunter." Her voice quivered. "I'm so very glad nothing happened to you or our children. God is truly generous in His grace and mercy. I don't know what we'd do, what I'd do if…" the older woman's words sank into silence. Marnie understood.

"God bless you, Mother Masterson. Please don't fret. We're all fine. Even Sister Rucker will be back singing soprano in the choir in no time. Yes, God is truly generous. More than we deserve." Marnie

149

thought about what a beloved place Bethlehem would be if they could be so caring all of the time. *Maybe the Communion phrase 'as often as you do this' had many meanings?* She promised to help make it so. Marnie felt loved at Bethlehem that day. She also knew that her life was spared a second time. God had something for her to do.

Marnie used her key to open her parents' front door. Her favorite foods beckoned. She knew it was a culinary trap, but her growling stomach and salivating mouth moved her feet forward. "Mom, Dad, I'm here."

"Hi honey. We're in the kitchen," called her father. "Come on back." Marnie eased onto a leather stool at the granite countertop and began munching on salad fixings from a large bowl. Her dad was observing his wife complete her mise en place.

"How was church today?" Her mother's brow furrowed just slightly. "I hope you weren't too tired… after yesterday." She kissed Marnie's right cheek, gave her a tight hug, and then pushed her daughter at arm's length. "Let me look at you." She eyed Marnie from head to toe and finally mouthed, "So glad you're safe."

"I was a bit worried that today's church festivities might be a bit too much for you." Her father's right brow raised like Mr. Spock from Star Trek.

"Oh no," she immediately disagreed. "I've been surprisingly energized all day. Today's worship services were especially warm. To be honest, I was a bit surprised. Folks at Bethlehem can be a bit staid."

"You're preaching to the choir. Remember, I used to be their pastor." He rolled his eyes. "They can be quite subdued, even distant, but they are pretty good at showing affection when they want to. Even the MOBs." Marnie stared at him. Her mouth fell open.

"I know a few things about the rumor mill too, young lady." He winked. "Overall, they are good folks. Sometimes you don't appreciate what you have until you almost lose it." As he closed his sentence, he closed the gap between them with a hug.

"Dad," Marnie whined. "Stop it. I feel like Raggedy Anne."

"Well, you are my little ragdoll," he joked. They made small talk as Mrs. Hunter finished preparing dinner; Marnie helped her dset the table.

"Well, as promised, we've got all your favorites and a few surprises." Mrs. Hunter stuck out her chest as she appraised her Sunday courses. "I took the liberty to also make those glazed carrots you like so much... and... red velvet cupcakes. I know that's your favorite too."

"Oh, no!" yelped Marnie.

"Oh, yes!" her mother replied. "We figured we'd watch a movie after dinner. One of your favorites," she promised. Dinner moved by much too quickly for Marnie as serving trays, plates, and utensils clicked amidst laughter and chatter. No one mentioned the bus incident. Marnie knew she'd eventually have to share details about that day with them, but not today.

After coffee and dessert, the three strolled leisurely into the den. "Thank you, gracious *chef*, for yet another splendid meal," daughter and husband almost said in unison. Mrs. Hunter's eyelids lowered. Marnie fell into the deep cushions of the loveseat across from the large television. Her legs dangled off the side of a huge multi-colored pillow. She instinctively grabbed a plush throw. Her dad found his place in his leather Barcalounger as Marnie's mother considered the shelves of DVDs. Like Marnie, both parents considered themselves film aficionados; they particularly loved the classics. Sometimes during movie night, it would take the family an hour and a huge bowl of popcorn to decide what to watch as they tried to convince each other of the merits of a particular film.

"Well Marnie, what will it be?" Her mother paused and waved her hands toward the shelved DVDs. "What do you have a taste for tonight? We have *all* your favorites. Would you like to see *The Magnificent Seven*, *From Hell to Texas*, *Sense and Sensibility*, or *My Left Foot*? On the other hand, maybe you'd like to watch an oldie, but a goodie… say, *Casablanca*, *It's a Wonderful Life*, *Citizen Kane* or *All About Eve*? Of course, if you're in the mood for more religious fare, we could watch *The Greatest Story Ever Told* or *The Robe*. I know the *Song of Bernadette* is your all-time favorite." They laughed at their inside joke as Rev. Hunter gazed back and forth between them. "I'm partial to *Spartacus*," said Mrs. Hunter.

"So many great movies, so little time," her dad sniggered.

"I just don't know, Mom. It's so hard to choose." Marnie scratched her head and unconsciously rubbed her left elbow. The latter gesture wasn't lost on either of her parents. After a few moments of silence, Marnie decided. "*The Magnificent Seven* it is. You can't go wrong with a good western. I always love the ending when Chico is riding away with Yul Brenner and Steve McQueen. Then he slowly looks at them. They all understand his unspoken decision and farewell. Chico then guides his horse back toward the village and the woman he loves!" Marnie kicked her feet in glee.

"Stop," exclaimed her mother. "Don't tell us the ending!" They could no longer contain their laughter. Several hours and several bowls of popcorn later, Marnie kissed and hugged her parents goodbye and grudgingly made her way out the front door. Her mother called out. "Let's have family dinner more than once a month, honey. Remember, *as often as you do this*."

"Love you!" both parents said unison, looked at each other, and chuckled. Would Marnie ever have someone she knew so well that they would speak in unison and complete each other's sentences? Would Jeremy be that person? Of all the men Marnie knew, save her father, she trusted Jeremy the most. Had he not proved his unfailing commitment to her? Then why was she stalling?

"Be sure to call us when you get home," Her mother quietly commanded as she waved at her daughter's back.

"Will do, Mom. Thanks for a great dinner and the company. All my favs. Love you so much." She would have to remember to call them once she got to Jeremy's.

Thirty minutes later, Marnie was snuggling deeper into the crook of Jeremy's left shoulder, her arms intertwined around the girth of his mid-section. She exhaled. *This day just can't get any better.*

They alternated visits to each other's homes, so Marnie met Jeremy at his townhouse. She loved his place. Old books lined shelves and a tattered

Navaho rug rested in front of a well-worn, rust-colored tweed sofa. Marnie was now getting lost on that very sofa. His walls teemed with mementos from many trips abroad, including artwork from Beijing that he gingerly maneuvered on the nineteen hour flight home, a Zimbabwean tapestry, a bronze statue from Sao Paolo, tiny Burmese figurines, and postcards from every U.S. city his curiosities took him. Because he knew she collected them, Jeremey brought Marnie a tiny cross from his destinations. It warmed her heart to know that, no matter where he was in the world, Jeremy was thinking about her. The crackling fire that was slowly dying didn't conjure up troubling images for her. Jeremy's presence smothered any such concerns. He drew her even closer to his chest. *I'm blessed with a sexy librarian boyfriend!*

Jeremy brushed his lips across her forehead. "I know why you didn't return my call last night. You thought I would nag you for getting wrangled by Donaldson again — this time into driving that damn bus yesterday. Yes, I was furious. I still am now, but not at you. Marn, I don't ever want you to avoid me for fear of some type of reprimand." He gazed deep into the flickering embers, then at the top of her forehead. He kissed her lightly there. "I am not your boss or your dad. I'm not going all Cro-Magnon on you, but here goes. I'm your man... and your partner. I'm always here for you. No matter what." He spoke just above a hush.

He brushed his lips across her forehead again. "I was terrified when I got your call about the accident. Then I saw the footage on the news. I shudder to think what could've happened. Then I remembered what you always say, 'No need to worry until you have to.' I knew that God was looking out for you. As usual, you were looking out for everyone else." His arms and his words warmed Marnie. "I see how you give one hundred and ten percent. I love that about you. I don't get why you're so driven. I know you want to give God your best. I get that. That's how I try to live too, but I think your drive opens you up to get overworked and underappreciated." His right palm grazed her left breast.

"Let's just think about the last year." Sensing his rising irritation, Marnie caressed his chest. His voice leveled, but he continued to summarize her work inventory. "You're single-handedly organizing this city-wide Family and Friends thing. I can't even count the number of times you've stood in for Pastor Donaldson at a meeting, to preach, or to teach. Clearly, he just loves to be around you." Marnie sensed an emerging green-eyed monster. She squeezed Jeremy's muscular frame tighter. "So to me, yesterday's fiasco is just another example in a long line of offenses." Jeremy repositioned himself so he could look directly into her eyes. "Marnie, just because you *can* do something doesn't mean you *should* do it. Sometimes it's okay to just say *no*. Sometimes it's okay just to be okay. I, I, I don't want to lose you." Marnie felt his body quiver. They found each other's mouths, as the embers turned from shades of red, orange, and yellow to ebony and gray.

"Your independence would probably scare most guys, but it's what drew me to you. You're your own woman. I love that about you. I just want you to be at peace in your career and, more importantly, in your life." His gaze took in her face again. "I

155

don't agree with Percy or Siobhan that Pastor Donaldson is using you. You would never allow that. You're working for God and not for Donaldson anyway. However, I don't think your gifts are being maximized either. Your joy is dying a slow death due to fatigue. You know what really concerns me, Marn?" He continued when he felt her nod against his chest. "Pastor Donaldson and that church, to a certain degree, disappoint you. They will probably continue to do so. 'People can't give you what they don't have.' You told me that a long time ago. So take your own advice. You somehow expect people to give you what you give them. Sadly, most folks rarely do. I think that if each of us finds a few people in our lifetimes to love us — I mean to truly love us — we are truly blessed." His mouth found hers again. "I'm not ashamed to say you are at the top of my list." Jeremy caressed her face with his eyes. She snuggled even closer. "Marn, are you sleep?" He didn't want to disturb their perfect position.

As she lay in Jeremy's obliging arms, Marnie begrudgingly admitted that few weeks passed without Pastor Donaldson assigning her some major project. Few days passed when she hadn't fallen asleep at her desk as the sun took its rest and she toiled to finish those same projects. Sometimes that sleep provided escape from dreams about Big Ed, but no real rest. Except for the church custodian, Marnie's car was usually the first automobile in the church parking lot and the last one to leave. But how could she find balance among all the people she loves, all the things she loves, and all the things she loves to do? God comes first. However, she knew that no one could work themselves closer to God. That's foolhardy. Our best is like filthy rags. *The truth will make you free.* Was everyone free except Marnie? Everyone she loved and everyone who loved her was battling to break her out of her self-imposed prison of perfection. Everyone but Marnie. She couldn't break free from the flames flicking around her face, smells of charring flesh, cut and singed elbows and arms, and Big Ed's curses and cries. *Whom Christ has made free, is free indeed.* Marnie would have to break free.

"I hear you, babe," Marnie purred. *We should do this more often.*

PART III

Chapter 17:

Life for Those Left Behind!

Could the memory of one of Marnie's first challenges as a young minister help her escape her current one? Could her past help her imagine a better present and future? Marnie volunteered during seminary to build houses for the poor in Chile and teach English as a second language in the Brazilian countryside. She received as much as she gave. However, she learned that she could serve the needy in her very own backyard. Her most memorable service was a stint in a tiny, rural Appalachian town ravaged by the exodus of the coal mining industry.

One of the relatively more affluent older residents, Mrs. Oxland, hosted Marnie. Well over sixty years old, Mrs. Oxland was a striking brown-haired woman with high cheekbones and riveting green eyes. An ivory cane was her third leg, but it didn't prevent her regale gate through town. "I'm a retired teacher. My husband died a slow, painful death from lung disease from working in that mine. Yet we were together over forty lovely years. God is still good." In return, for what she referred to as 'God's manifold blessings,' Mrs. Oxland welcomed missionaries into her home each year. Marnie initially wondered how she could live on the fifty dollars a month stipend from the seminary. Compared to most Lowellville residents, she was a millionaire.

Marnie was the minister in training for five months at the Lowellville Congregational Church. Her responsibilities included preaching twice a month, teaching Sunday school, and leading a weekly young adult bible class. However, her primary role was teaching math at Bing Young, the local elementary school. She was excited and a bit nervous, but was warmly welcomed by the principal, five other teachers, and twenty infectious grins who greeted her daily at the underfunded school.

Mrs. Oxland helped Marnie acclimate to the local culture. Most residents abandoned the town long ago. The rest of the tiny tight-knit community hung on for dear life. Most were friendly and welcomed the stranger. The female minister intrigued others in the somewhat conservative, incestuous town. Marnie adjusted quickly and made amazing strides with her tiny charges.

One hazy Saturday morning, Marnie sat in a weatherworn lounge chair on Mrs. Oxland's back porch journaling about her week's experiences and her upcoming sermon. She was grateful for the respite from the crowds she drew and cherished the time to reflect. Mrs. Oxland rushed through the screen door.

Marnie asked, "What wrong, ma'am?"

"Minister Hunter, I'm so sorry to interrupt your quiet time, but I need your help."

"Yes, yes, Mrs. Oxland. What do you need?" Marnie's forehead furrowed.

"It's not about me. It's about Teddy. You know, the young man who tends my yard."

Marnie met Teddy soon after arriving in Lowellville and liked him instantly. His petite frame and larger than life personality drew her. Although Mrs. Oxland cautioned them more than once about chatting while Teddy was working, the two young people sought each other out for animated conversations about their lives and the bible. The sandy blond-headed man's tattered clothes and hole-ridden shoes evidenced his family's poverty; his lawn care business was vital to their survival. "I like being able to take care of my family. Folks call me an entrepreneur. I just like to eat." Teddy laughed. "My grades weren't good enough to get in college. I started with dead-end jobs. Then I found my calling. Flowers and plants love me!"

He wasn't exaggerating. Mrs. Oxland's front yard hosted swaths of anemones, Dutchman's breeches, freesias, and daffodils. As if competing, her backyard bloomed wild violets, native orchids, white Oconee, and toothworts. Rows of Red Eastern redbud trees shaded all these eye-catching blooms. The elderly woman proudly took credit and the town's people nodded and humored her boasts about specialized fertilizer. They knew it was Teddy's handiwork.

Both Mrs. Oxland and Marnie were concerned because the usually punctual young man missed his last weekly appointment. *The weather was unusually humid; maybe he was playing hooky in the nearby water hole,* Marnie thought. Now Mrs. Oxland's concern-riddled face suggested otherwise. "It's Teddy. He just showed up here hysterical." After a pregnant pause, the elderly woman stuttered, "His grandmother died." No further words were necessary.

Teddy's grandmother was his primary caregiver. Granny, as he affectionately called her, reared him since he was two years old. They still lived together with several of his siblings, cousins, and an aunt with Down syndrome. The household eked by on Granny's pension check, Teddy's lawn care business, and odd jobs the industrious young man was able to find. High blood pressure and diabetes whittled away at Granny's body, but even arthritis couldn't prevent her from cooking for her family each day. "Like it says in the bible, I'm blessed. More than most around here." Teddy's sunny outlook reminded Marnie about what was important in life. During one of their many chats, Teddy poked out his chest and said, "She used to take care of me. Now I take care of Granny."

Mrs. Oxland continued. "Teddy showed up today for work apologizing for being absent, but too upset to really work. I can barely understand him. I don't know what to do. Would you please talk with him?" the older woman beseeched Marnie.

"Of course, ma'am. Of course I will," the somewhat frightened intern responded. Mrs. Oxland led Teddy into the room and looked back over her shoulder at the forlorn lad as she exited. Marnie motioned for him to sit in the sturdy, threadbare chair across from her. "I'm so very sorry to hear about your grandmother, Teddy. I know you loved her very much."

He hastily wiped away tears. "Thank you so much, Minister Marnie." He choked back sobs. Words stuck in his throat. He gulped and slowly continued, "Miss Marnie, I just don't know what I'm gonna do. I just

don't know. What am I gonna do without Granny?"
He searched Marnie's eyes for direction. This was
her first time counseling someone about death. All
of her classroom training and practices seemed
somehow hollow.

"Teddy." She reached out and hugged him. "I
want to help."

He started to sob again. "Miss Marnie, no one
can help me now. It's just too much. Granny was
fine yesterday morning. We ate breakfast together
like we always do. I told her my work schedule for
the day like I always do. She told me to stay out of
trouble like she always does. Just like any other day.
Then I went to work." He paused so long Marnie
thought he'd passed out. "Then one of my friends
came to find me to tell me that Granny... had...
had a heart attack. They took her to the hospital.
We don't have no insurance. I got there as fast as I
could, but it was too late... I didn't even get a
chance to say goodbye."

A round of gut-wrenching moans followed the
tragic summary. Haphazardly wiping the back of his
right hand across his face only smeared tears and
mucus. Marnie pressed a handful of tissues into his
hand. "I'm so sorry, Miss Marnie. I don't want to be
a burden, but I just don't know what to do. I didn't
know where to go either, so I came here. Miss
Oxland can always tell me what to do." His voice
trailed as Marnie stroked his hands. Teddy cried,
"My Granny is dead and I will *never* see her again."
His entire body yielded to the full weight of that
awareness.

God help me say the right words and do the right thing.
"Teddy, I know how you feel. My grandmother

163

passed away a few years ago. She was one of my best friends. It really hurt. I still miss her today. However, I know I will see her again one day in heaven. Just like you will see your Granny again one day in heaven. We will be together again with them one day in heaven." Teddy's body reeled backward and he wailed uncontrollably again. Marnie's words meant to bring peace not pain.

"No, no." He shook his head back and forth with abandon. "I won't even see her again then. Granny was a Christian. I'm not. She took me to church every Sunday. I believe in God and Jesus, but I never went down there to talk to the preacher. You know, to say I wanted to be a Christian. Now it's too late." Teddy placed his head in his hands and rounded his upper body between his legs. *God help him.*

"Teddy, it doesn't have to be that way. You can still see your Granny again one day in heaven. You said you believe. All you have to do is say so."

The young man raised his head ever so slightly. "What do you mean? How?" he quietly queried.

Marnie explained what he needed to do to establish a personal relationship with God through Jesus Christ. Her eyes rolled upward as she tried to recall what her father said every Sunday. "Do you believe in God?" she asked.

"Yes," Teddy said.

"Do you believe that Jesus Christ was God's son?" she continued.

"Yes," he said.

"Do you believe that Jesus Christ lived, died, and rose from the grave as a sacrifice for us for all times?

"Yes, Minister Marnie. I believe," Teddy said.

"Then pray with me," she said. Together they said a short prayer of repentance. "Teddy, you did it. That's all it takes. You're saved and you will see Granny again one day in heaven." She paused to stroke his hair. "However, I won't lie to you. This won't take the pain you're feeling right now away. It will get better overtime; God will make your heart hurt a little less each day. I promise. I'm sure Mrs. Oxland will help too." Marnie's simple words about salvation and what it meant for Teddy and his grandmother soothed him in a way she'd never witnessed before or expected. No big words. No grand gestures. No pretense. Just a quiet conversation about God's love and sacrifice.

Marnie prayed that Teddy would rely on God, his family, and a local church, during the painful days sure to come without his grandmother. "Thank you so much, Minister Marnie. Thank you." Teddy lowered his eyes. It was Marnie's first time ministering to someone who accepted Christ. She would never forget it. This was what her calling meant. *Thank you, God, for enabling me to serve.*

Mrs. Oxland was standing outside the door and overheard the entire conversation. She tiptoed in and rubbed Teddy's unkempt curls. "Teddy, I am so glad you came here. It's going to be all right. I love you."

Several minutes later, Teddy was devouring a cheese sandwich and drinking chocolate milk at Mrs. Oxland's kitchen table as they discussed funeral arrangements. "My family can't even afford to bury Granny." Shame welled up in his eyes.

The two women glanced at each other. "Teddy, don't worry. Marnie and I will pay for the funeral."

The young man cried again. "We'll make all the arrangements. Don't worry; just be sure to tell your family." Several days later, Mrs. Oxland and Marnie flanked Teddy on a front church pew, each holding one of his shaking hands, as he said goodbye to his beloved Granny. "Thanks… for sitting with me." His voice quivered. The three of them attended church together every Sunday during the remainder of Marnie's time in Lowellville.

She kept up with Teddy through letters with Mrs. Oxland several times a year. When the older woman died Marnie lost touch with Teddy. However, she still included him by name in her nightly prayers. Despite the passage of time, Marnie remembered how God first used her to provide comfort to a young man. Teddy was saved spiritually. Marnie wondered about the life of another young man, Lil' Ed.

Chapter 18:

Confrontations and Callings

Did Marnie hate Big Ed? She imagined him spewing sexist statements, racial epithets, homophobic tirades, and xenophobic slurs to anyone within earshot. He wasn't the kind of man you wanted to meet alone on a dark road. Nevertheless, did he deserve to die the way he did? Was his death in an inferno payback for the hell he likely put anyone through who was different from him? In his youth, did he bully smaller kids on the playground, refer to girls as bitches if they refused to let him get past second base, or break the windows out of people's houses from *that* part of town. Her gut told her that Big Ed had not amassed any Boy Scout badges. Did biblical warnings finally catch up with him in the person of Minister Marnie Hunter? *Touch not my anointed and do my prophet no harm.* Yet scripture could indict Marnie too. Was she just making excuses to justify her actions and inactions?

No, Marnie didn't wish Big Ed dead, but she was uncertain exactly how she felt and that uncertainty was tearing her apart. Preachers needed to be certain. Pastors don't have the latitude to be unsure about how they feel about people, even people who are unloving and seemingly unlovable. What if God saw Marnie that way? No matter how she spun it, she knew that ministers served everyone! Jesus was not a respecter of persons. Neither could she. She rubbed the bruises on her elbows. They were constant reminders of her *truth*, of a multitude of scars and a mental impasse to her future as a minister.

Marnie pulled her car into the familiar lot. The place looked exactly as it did when she sped in years ago frantically searching for directions. The same two rusty gas pumps, low-hanging Gas-N-Snack sign, and semi-paved drive greeted her. Marnie fought back the dread rising in her gut. No. No. If she ever hoped to help other people as a minister, she would have to start by helping herself. *Physician heal thyself.* Easier said than done. As she opened the cloudy glass door filled with frayed fliers, the same grizzled-faced attendant greeted Marnie.

"Hey, Missy," Jackson said. "Long time no see. Never thought I'd see *you* again. Most visitors don't come back. Glad to see you're all right. Heard about that accident, 'bout what happened to Big Ed and Lil' Ed. Just terrible. They say you saved the boy's life! Rescues like that just don't happen 'round here." Marnie nodded and waited for her turn to enter the one-sided conversation.

"It's good to see you too, Jackson. I'm well. Yes, it's been a long time." Marnie liked the friendly old man, but she was on a mission. No time for small talk. "I'm actually here about Lil' Ed. I'm trying to find out where his family lives to hopefully talk to his mother." Her voice slowed.

"Lil' Ed still lives with his Ma. His Pa's death hit the family real hard." Marnie gulped hard, trying to swallow the rising guilt. "They're making it. A miracle that both of 'em weren't burned up in that crash — if not for you." Marnie averted her eyes from this praise. Would the old man's gratitude change if he knew the truth? The scars on her elbows throbbed.

As Marnie was about to leave the gas station for what she believed would likely be the last time, Jackson stuttered. "You know Missy, it's strange how things turn out. I remember that night." He looked toward the cobwebs dangling from the ceiling. "I remember what happened here. Big Ed, he was outta line — way outta line. After you dashed outta here, he went on and on. I tried to calm him down but wasn't no stopping him when he got like that. Everyone 'round here knew it. He was the best mechanic and farmer in this town, but..." Jackson stalled. "That night, He was coming... for you. I just knew it. He was so fired up! Hate makes you do that. Jumped in that old truck and headed down Rick Road — opposite direction from his house but a short cut to the highway. Trying to cut you off, I guess. I knew he was coming after you. Just prayed you would make it to the highway and be long gone. Strange how things turned out, you saving Lil' Ed and all. Strange how things turned out." Jackson was now whispering. Their exchange ended as quickly as it had started. Jackson glanced at the smudged front store window and out across the gravel road. A faint smile crossed his face. "You have a good day now, Missy."

The old man's directions were perfect. Despite minimal signage and meandering roads, Marnie finally found the gravel trail. After driving several more country miles, the faded blue shotgun house emerged. Marnie slowed as she approached the shack. It had seen better days, but she felt welcomed by the smattering of daffodils that flanked its wooden steps. Her resolve ebbed the closer she got to the patio door. Was this a good idea? Maybe some things should be left alone. Maybe her presence would cause more harm than good. She clinched her fingers. She knew that this conversation, this confrontation, was inevitable. *The fervent, effectual prayers of the righteous availeth much. Pray without ceasing.* She silently prayed.

Marnie rapped on the wooden portion of the crooked screen door. She heard the sounds from a television, dogs barking, and faint footfalls. She knocked again. "Yes," a low, raspy voice called from a semi-dark hallway. "Can I help you?" Marnie came face to face with the pretty, gaunt face of the woman she knew was Little Ed's mother and Big Ed's widow. "Can I help you?" the dirty blond woman queried again as she peeped out of a large tear in the wire mesh.

"Uh, hi," Marnie stuttered. "I'm looking for the wife, uh, I mean the widow of a man called Ed, Big Ed. Do you know her?" Marnie already knew the answer to her question, but waiting for the response gave her time to gather the courage to continue.

"Yes, that's me. Ed was my husband. I'm Clarice Fountain." She asked again, "Can I help you?"

"Yes. My name is Marnie Hunter. Jackson from the gas station said I could find you here. You don't know me, but I need to talk to you." Marnie hoped her pleading voice and sullen eyes would help her gain access. Clarice eyed Marnie up and down.

"Sure, come in." The slight young woman sighed.

Marnie immediately had second thoughts as she entered the porch. Her mind raced. No one actually knew she was there. If something happened to her, it would take weeks before someone could retrace her tracks — if ever. They wouldn't even know where to start. Her parents and friends thought she was spending a quiet weekend at home. What if Clarice was like Ed? What if Ed was the unwilling student rather than a willing leader? What if he learned his bigoted beliefs from his beguiling romantic partner? Marnie slowly stepped through the door.

Clarice wore a washed-out yellow cotton shirt that buttoned up the front, blue jean capris pants that were similarly faded, and red flip-flops. Her face was pale with no make-up and the humidity caused strands of her blond hair to frame her rose-colored oval cheeks. Despite the cigarette in her hand and creases around her eyes, Clarice's face was almost angelic. A pack of Marlboros poked out of her shirt pocket.

Marnie scanned the entry. Three rusty, steel rocking chairs perched on the sparsely decorated porch. A wire screen wrapped around the entire space, seamlessly bound by wooden planks. The wooden floor of the porch creaked with every step the minister took. Clarice pointed toward the second yellow rocker and Marnie eased into it. "I sit out here when I smoke." She seemed to want Marnie to understand why she hadn't invited her inside the house. Clarice glanced at her visitor's crisp, white shirt, khaki linen skirt, pearl bud earrings and matching necklace, modest flats, and leather purse. She flushed and looked toward the wooden floor. Marnie knew that honesty seldom emerges in strained situations, so she immediately reached across the chasm toward Clarice.

"Thank you so much for your time. I hope you aren't busy," Marnie said.

Clarice spoke between puffs. "No, I got a little time. My boy will be home in a few minutes. I know who you are. I figured you'd come... eventually."

Marnie then walked across the chasm. "You did? Why?"

Clarice spoke in clips between cigarette drags. "At the hospital I was told that a lady was at the accident. Saved my boy. At the time, I was so focused on Lil' Ed. Scared he wouldn't make it. He laid there so quiet and small. So much blood. I couldn't stop screaming. The nurses probably spent more time quieting me than tending to him. I knew his Pa was dead. Died at the scene. All burned up. I just couldn't lose Lil' Ed." Clarice choked on her words as she returned to that the night that irrevocably conjoined and changed all their lives. "I was told the lady wasn't from around here," Clarice spoke as if sharing a secret. "I was just so focused on my boy. I wasn't much of a churchgoer, but I prayed so much that night. Promised God that if He saved my boy, I'd change my ways. Don't know whether we can make deals with God, but I tried. I would've done anything to save my boy. Just prayed and prayed. Seven days later, Lil' Ed woke up. I know it was a miracle. Don't care what those doctors say about him healing while he was sleeping in that coma. I know God did it."

Clarice's breathing was barely palpable. Marnie sat quietly, taking in the story from the mother's perspective. "By the time I thought about finding your hospital room, you were already gone. I wanted to thank you for saving my boy. God knows I did." Clarice hands shook as she took a long drag on a second cigarette and flicked the ash out the screen. Marnie instinctively reached out and rubbed her shoulder. The young mother didn't pull away. She continued to talk, as she looked heavenward, almost as if in a trance.

"Although I can't seem to kick these cigs, I've been going to church ever since. Made a promise to God and I intend to keep it. Going also helps me deal with Big Ed's death and the way he died. The life we led. God gave my son back to me and I am grateful — grateful to God and to you." Marnie chocked back a slight gasp as her own memories yanked her back to that night.

Clarice suddenly shifted in the rusty chair and looked directly at Marnie. "I can't thank you enough for my boy." Her eyes filled with tears. Marnie lost her composure.

"I'm... I'm so sorry about your husband, Clarice," Marnie stammered. "About his death... so very sorry." Marnie felt the warm tears flowing down her cheeks. She didn't wipe them away. They flowed as freely as her words. "Clarice, I came to talk to you. I wanted to talk to you about that night, about Big Ed, about why I didn't save him. You need to know. It was my fault. It was all my fault he died." There. Marnie said it. No matter what happened next, Marnie came clean. No more hiding. If the truth makes you free, Marnie finally began that long walk toward freedom. She didn't know how Clarice would respond, but Marnie knew she could deal with it. Clarice attempted to speak, but Marnie didn't stop.

"Clarice, please don't thank me. I don't deserve thanks. You just don't understand. I couldn't get the door open. I yanked and yanked, but it wouldn't budge." Marnie's body shook as she strained to control the pent-up sobs that were waiting for years to escape — to be free. Her body shuttered as she tried to explain that ill-fated night to Clarice, tried to make her understand why her husband burned to death. Marnie wanted to continue the confession, but her words choked from anguish and guilt. Clarice caressed Marnie's left shoulder and met her gaze in a gesture that suggested that she too had a history of hiding emotions and experiences for the good of others, but at great personal expense. At that moment, Marnie realized that Clarice had her own scars and crosses to bear.

"That night changed everything for all of us," Clarice said above a murmur. "Marnie, I wanna thank you for saving my son… and for saving me."

Marnie tried to share details about that night, not to burden the innocent mother's shoulders, but to share the truth she deserved. They were sitting less than a few inches from each other, but Marnie could barely see Clarice through the tears. "Clarice, you just don't understand," Marnie muttered and rubbed her elbows.

Clarice couldn't have been more than twenty-six years old, but her face reflected an eerie calm Marnie only saw among wizened church mothers who spent years depending and leaning on the Lord. It was a face of faith, hope, patience, and wisdom. "Big Ed... my husband was hard to know and hard to love. You saved my son. Saved me more than you know. That's all that matters." Marnie gazed deep into the young mother's eyes and understood her guarded message. Jackson's words and Clarice's cryptic comments confirmed that Big Ed's caustic reach had been long and wide. Their conversation ended abruptly as Lil' Ed barged through the door. Marnie quietly uttered, "No need to tell him about me." Clarice nodded.

"Young man, you know how I feel about running in the house." Clarice sent a small smile in his direction as he fidgeted at the door. "What do you say to visitors?"

Lil' Ed peeped up at Marnie and said in a small voice, "Nice to meet you, ma'am."

Just as swiftly as she spoke, he dashed into the house. Marnie's eyes rapidly followed the spry boy. The scarred lines running down the back of his legs matched those on her arms and elbows. He didn't need to know who she was. They were linked forever. That was enough. The rocker creaked as Clarice stood. Her thin lips curved up slightly. "Well, I better go feed him or he'll eat the couch cushions." Her rankling remarks couldn't hide her pride for her young son. "So glad you came, Marnie. God bless you. Please pray for me and I'll pray for you." Clarice extended her right hand. Marnie shook it, turned, and pushed the screen door wide.

Chapter 19:

The Truth Will Make You Free!

Ambling through her front door, bible, purse, and bloated book bag in hand, the young cleric pressed the black knob on the portable sound system and tumbled onto the sofa. The contents from her straining arms found their own destinations on and around the plush piece of furniture. As the music from her favorite homemade Meditation #1 CD filled the room, the cares of a hectic, but generally fulfilling day at church dropped away as easily as the bundle she had carried.

To anyone else, the compilation was a hodgepodge of artists and genres from across time. Marnie refused long ago to apologize or explain her eclectic tastes in music, art, and culture. The hymns, pop, spirituals, country, gospel, rhythm and blues she liked all had one common theme: inspirational, thought-provoking messages. "You Can't Always Get What You Want" by The Rolling Stones, Johnny Nash's "I Can See Clearly Now," Barry Manilow's "I Write the Songs," and Prince's "The Ladder" were just as uplifting to Marnie as John Newton's "Amazing Grace" or Cartwright's "The Old Ship of Zion." She was especially partial to any hymn by Johnny and June Cash or utterance from Karen Carpenter. The lyrics and harmonies of the motley mix were on par with the most eloquent sermon. These songs helped Marnie through the Big Ed incident. Now each day she felt a bit more reenergized.

As the lyrical litany continued, memories unfolded of her journey since accepting her calling at seven years old. The songs drew out images, sounds, events, laughter, tears, and people. Marnie just let her past flow over her like a flood because the messages from those experiences would guide crucial decisions moving forward. She fondly remembered Super Saint scampering through St. John's, her baptism, her father's sermons, Easter speeches, choirs singing, and Vacation Bible schools. Middle and high school provided the canvas on which other church events were drawn like flirting with boys in the Teen Ministry and outings to King's Island. College meant frequent trips home to participate in church musicals, Single's Ministry excursions, and her father's surprise twenty-fifth year pastoral appreciation party. She only grimaced slightly at mental images of seminary challenges; most caused her lips to curl upward.

Now thirty-something, Marnie was older. The decisions she made over the next few weeks would illustrate whether she was wiser. Her present position at Bethlehem wasn't all-bad. Marnie believed that Pastor Donaldson was an honest, ethical person committed to God and the community. He tended to delegate pastoral work rather than get his hands dirty. The delegating was killing Marnie! Things needed to change if she was to continue to serve there. She couldn't change how he pastored, but Marnie could change whether and how she accepted responsibilities. Whether she called them MOBs or not, Marnie was also tired of biased, opinionated churchwomen and their unchecked animus. Things had to change because she was changing. Marnie would no longer be a Shadow Pastor.

The start of her meeting with Pastor Donaldson the following day was predictable. It was their first meeting since the bus accident. Marnie counted on him to heap lavish praise on her. At least he wasn't stingy on that score. Pastor Donaldson was comfortable providing positive feedback and constructive criticism. He seemed genuinely impressed with Marnie's progress as Associate Minister. Her excellent work guaranteed more responsibilities. It was a crazy, vicious cycle that would soon end. "I just couldn't preach two sermons every Sunday and teach Sunday school when I do if it wasn't for you, Minister Hunter," he admitted. "I know there were some challenges this week, but you handled them well."

"Thank you, Pastor. I was glad that the services went well Sunday. I think Evangelist Romanoff's solo during first service prepared the congregation for your sermon. You know how difficult it can be to preach about tithing. Everyone seemed receptive and the trustees reported a twenty percent increase in the tithes and offerings over both last month and last year." The pastor nodded in agreement.

"Yes, Minister Romanoff's voice is truly a gift. Please suggest to the Minister of Music that she sing either a lead or a solo once a month." Marnie made a note of this action item. After completing her weekly update and informing him about the additional activities for the Family and Friends Festival, Marnie scribbled several new action items. She needed to prepare to preach at the 8:45 a.m. service on the fifth Sunday and locate a new Teen Class Sunday school teacher who yelled, "I'm done herding cats" as she dashed from the classroom. Marnie segued into last Sunday's confrontation. She was doing her best not to think about them as MOBs.

"Pastor, I appreciate how you trust me to handle conflicts that arise, but I was taken aback last Sunday when Mothers Masterson and Peters and Sister Right approached me after church. I felt ambushed. To be completely honest, their plan to establish a dress code or provide lap scarves and shawls to young women is ridiculous! You know how much effort it took to grow our young demographic. They are vital to Bethlehem's future. I can't gauge all their motives, but I just don't think the young women are being seductive. I just don't believe it. It's fashion to them." Pastor Donaldson listened and words continued to tumble from Marnie's mouth.

"They said you told them to talk to me. Like you, I was exhausted after a long day at church. I wouldn't presume to tell you how to pastor, but I just wish it had been handled differently. I love ministry, but I get tired too. There seems to be some belief that I don't get weary in well doing. I have a life outside of Bethlehem Church too." Marnie exhaled. "The opportunities here at Bethlehem have enabled me to hone my teaching, preaching, and administrative skills. However, to be completely honest, Pastor, I am feeling overworked and underappreciated. There are seven other gifted ministers at Bethlehem. It does them a disservice when the brunt of their responsibilities are to sit in the pulpit on Sunday mornings and sporadically provide input during bible class — when they decide to attend." Marnie wanted to avoid sounding bitter. She wasn't the least bit bitter, just resolute. Pastor Donaldson avoided eye contact and twiddled a Mont Blanc pen on his desk.

"I've reached an impasse. Ministry here has largely become a series of projects, events, and activities not assigned decently and in order. This barrage is draining my joy! What I believe to be differences in the workload and expectations for the male and female ministers most troubles me." Marnie was on a roll. Super Saint would be proud. "Take the bus accident. Like me, Minister Mark Barber has a chauffer's license. Like me, he was supposed to chaperone the event. He was a no show. Who does that? What allowed him to believe he could do that? I can't speak to whether, how, or *if* you addressed the matter with him. Sunday he couldn't even make eye contact with me. Yet when all is said and done, he wasn't there." After another long pause, she uttered, "Pastor, neither were you." Marnie's heart was racing, but gender inequality was at the heart of her concerns about her future at Bethlehem.

"In many ways, Bethlehem is eons ahead of most local churches in terms of promoting gender parity and inclusivity. We still have a long way to go. We might be patting ourselves on the back too soon at the expense of other needed improvements. It is very important to me that I serve in a place that is making a concerted effort to foster equality on all fronts in terms of class, gender, race, sexual orientation, and any other way that the world tries to divide us." There, she said it. Marnie spilled the beans. *I can kiss ordination goodbye.* Pastor Donaldson cleared his throat, took a sip from the mug on his desk, and finally spoke.

"Minister Hunter, first and foremost, I want to thank you for all that you do here at Bethlehem. As I've told you so many times, you continue to make an indelible mark on every dimension of this congregation. You continue in the great history of service begun by your parents here. I think that even your father would agree that you are exceeding his legacy in many ways. Once ordained, I know you will continue this tradition in ways that even I can't imagine." *I guess I'm still an ordination candidate.* His brow wrinkled as if he was trying to decide which issue to address first. "First, I'm so sorry, about Mother Masterson and her crew." Marnie stopped her mouth from falling open when he referred to them that way. Maybe he knew more than she thought. "You are right. I should've told them to make an appointment with me rather than sending them your way. It was wrong of me. Don't worry. We won't be doling out any lap scarves or shawls as long as I'm the pastor." Marnie breathed a sigh of relief.

"I am so distressed that you feel unappreciated and overworked. I have noticed your long hours and that you seem fatigued more often than not. I apologize for not saying anything and for not intervening. To be honest, I rely on you so much because… I can. So part of this dilemma is due to selfishness on my part. Another part is due to expediency. That's what happened with the Fun Land trip. I thought to myself, 'I should be on that bus, but Marnie can handle it.' You did. However, you shouldn't have done it alone. I shudder to think what could have happened and that I wasn't there." His lips trembled. "No excuse will suffice." The pastor shifted in his chair. "Although I know I should begin to train the other ministers more concertedly, it has just been easier to continue with things the way they are. It's not right and I will change it." He had difficulty looking Marnie directly in her eyes.

He sipped from the mug on his desk and cleared his throat again. She could see sweat beads on his forehead. "Minister Hunter, the issue about gender disparity is really hard to hear. I've prided myself on trying to be fair to all the ministers and the entire membership. Again, I know I have higher expectations for you and maybe for a few others." He didn't mention names and Marnie didn't ask. "We all know it still exists in our denomination, but I don't want a good ole boys network here." His voiced quieted, but he continued. "You know Marnie, I didn't always think as I do now about women in ministry. You and people like you convinced me to think differently. I saw your dedication to God and people, your sacrificial spirit, and the way you strive to treat everyone fairly. Women like you made the difference and changed my mind. However, I still have a long way to go. I admit that." He cleared his throat again.

"You are the Associate Minister for a reason. You do such an excellent job! You get things done! I like things to get done and get done well. No excuse, but an honest explanation for my actions." Marnie nodded. "I know you won't always be here. God has much bigger and better things for you to do. I would never hold you back. I hope you believe me when I say that I only mean you well." His voice slowed again. "Marnie,

I am truly sorry for any hurt or harm that I have directly or indirectly caused you. Please charge it to my head and not my heart. I need your help to make it right."

Marnie and Pastor Donaldson brainstormed about ways she could continue to fulfill certain church responsibilities that were important to her and valuable to the congregation. They also talked about which tasks to delegate to other clergy. He promised to begin weekly training sessions with the other clergy without Marnie's assistance. "Marnie, why don't you create your own job description so we can work together to get this right." She nodded and jotted a note on her pad.

"Pastor Donaldson, I have two related requests. I would like to have a regular workday, from 9:00 a.m. to 5:00 p.m., unless an emergency requires additional time." He agreed. "I'd also like a day off during the week. I'm on duty all day each Sunday. So I've actually been working six-day workweeks since I started here."

"Yes, yes. Let's put them both in place immediately." Pastor Donaldson nodded.

"Thank you, Pastor," she said.

"Marnie, we have talked about quite a few issues today. I'm sure others things will come up as we formalize these changes. I don't want this to be the last time we talk this candidly. Please come to me at any time with concerns, critiques, and suggestions. I welcome your insight. Although I pride myself on being a forward thinker, I'm growing too. I really want to promote equality and inclusion." Marnie's beamed at his final comment. Their meeting lasted over two hours. Time well spent.

Marnie strutted out of Pastor Donaldson's office, chest out, and chin held high. She believed he was a man of his word. Only time would tell. She was prepared to respond either way. More importantly, Marnie directly confronted the issues that nagged her so long. She stuck her chest out even further and raised her chin higher. Marnie knew that she would still have to push back against the *Big Eds* in her world, male and female, who would try to silence her voice, control her behavior, and squash her dreams. She would. Marnie supporters, both family and friends, were God sent, but only she could safeguard her beliefs, dreams, time, resources and her heart. She would.

Marnie's confidence that her pastor was true to his word increased when, several days later, he instituted two administrative changes. "After reviewing salary ranges for ministers in similar posts, I was shocked and ashamed to learn that you were making about ten thousand dollars less than your peers annually," Pastor Donaldson exclaimed. "The raise will take effect immediately and retroactively." *Thank you, God*, Marnie thought. Secondly, he created a diversity task force. Although he welcomed Marnie's input, Pastor Donaldson would spearhead the group and ensure that it implemented action items to foster increased equity and inclusivity at Bethlehem. "Marnie, I take the verse in the sentence prayer, *thy kingdom come*, very seriously. Working together, I know we can help bring all the beauty and wonder we imagine about God's kingdom to our church and hopefully beyond." Marnie knew she wouldn't serve at Bethlehem forever. God had bigger and better things for her to do — things that even she couldn't imagine. For now, her ministry would be much more enjoyable and empowering. For now, she would blossom where she was planted.

Chapter 20:

Coming Out of the Shadows

You can't always get what you want,
You can't always get what you want,
You can't always get what you want,
But if you try sometimes, well you just might find...
You get what you need!

Marnie grooved around the furniture in her modest living room as one of her favorite songs floated through the space. She mumbled the second verse, gyrating her hips and snapping her fingers as she mimicked Mick Jagger. The chorus was her cue to sing out. She especially loved the back-up choir and raised her hands as their 'ooh's and 'aah's crescendoed. Marnie believed that the Rolling Stones must have been having church when they recorded that tune. It was a rock & roll sermon for the masses. Rev. Jagger was preaching directly to Marnie. It may have taken her a few years, but she was finally listening!

It was time to trust God fully. It was time to trust the people in her life fully. If she ever expected to embrace her calling as the preacher and eventually the pastor she knew she would be, Marnie must share her deepest secret with the people she cared about the most. The next gathering of the Seminary Sisters took place at Monica's house. Marnie was glad because, of all her friends' homes, she felt safest there. The over-sized, gray-blue colored sectional sofa hugged you. Throw pillows lay around the room. A brown faux-mink coverlet lay atop the bay window seat, beckoning visitors to come enjoy the scenic view of the babbling brook and farmland out back. Her friends eyed each other when Marnie poured her third glass; they knew something was up. She was a one glass of wine kind of girl.

Marnie gazed out the bay window and spoke in hushed tones. Her three friends leaned forward hanging onto her every word. Several hours later, Marnie said, "So that's the whole story. That's where these scars on my arms came from. That's why I've seemed so rattled sometimes. I wanted to tell you all, but I just couldn't. It's taken me all this time to fully wrap my brain around the experience." She scratched her right elbow. "I only told Dad last year. I've been so guilty and tormented. Sometimes I thought I was losing my mind. Now you know." Several moments passed before Monica spoke.

"I'm so sorry Marnie. So sorry you carried that burden all these years. I wish you'd told us sooner. I don't know, but I would like to think that we could have somehow made it better for you. However, I don't know that. What matters is that you told us when you could. I'm grateful for that."

"You did what you could in a terrible, terrible situation. Marnie, you saved a boy's life! You put yourself in danger in the process. The police realized that. Clarice did too. You have nothing to feel guilty about." Percy leaned forward and caressed Marnie's cheek. Siobhan interjected.

"Marn, I can't imagine what I would have done if I were in your shoes. You're like some kind of Super Saint. You can't spend your life thinking about shoulda, woulda, coulda. It will eat you alive," said her flaming-haired friend.

"Nobody here will ever admit it, but I will. That's just one less bigot in the world." Percy smirked. Both Monica and Siobhan darted their eyes toward her. "What? I don't care. Roll your eyes at me all you want." Percy scolded. "The truth shall make us free. You know I'm telling the truth. Why should Marnie spend an iota of time or energy worrying about that creep? She's been literally wasting away little by little all these years worry about a guy who would have sooner raped her and left her like strange fruit as talk to her. Good riddance, I say."

Marnie said, "Percy, that's not the point. It's not about who Big Ed was. It's about who I am and who I am trying to model. *What would Jesus do*? Remember?"

Percy looked away in defiance. "So what? What if somewhere deep, deep in the recesses of Marnie's mind, in the depths of her subconscious, she didn't do all she could to save that monster? So what! I tell you, she did more than I would have. She's a saint, I say."

Monica's final dagger in Percy's direction silenced the hotheaded ally. Percy's words hit home with Marnie. Although pointed and somewhat graceless, they encapsulated exactly what Marnie feared all those years.

Marnie cried, "How can I get ordained next month or ever and prepare for lifelong ministry if I harbor ill will against anyone? Or if I didn't do all I could for someone — even someone like Big Ed?" Marnie began to rub both elbows rhythmically this time.

Monica gripped her hands and held them firmly, as if to finally break Marnie's troubling ritual. "Stop it, Marnie! Stop it now! No more self-hatred. No more self-doubt. No more tearing yourself up inside. It stops now!"

"Sorry, Marnie. Don't listen to me. You know I'm still healing from divorce. I have issues with pushy men." Percy lowered her eyes and backtracked.

Monica continued. "Percy's just talking to be talking. She's speaking about what she *might* have done. Even that's conjecture. Percy is wrong. You know why? Because that's not you. We all know you. I know that we are all women of God, but you are different. We all know that, out of all of us, you have the deepest capacity to love unconditionally, to forgive immediately, and to expect the best from others, no matter who they are. Out of all of us, you have the biggest heart. You have the least guile of anyone I have ever met." The other two women nodded in agreement. Monica held Marnie's tear-stained face and looked directly into her bloodshot eyes. "Marnie, you did all you could." Then Monica embraced her best friend; the two other women completed the circle of healing.

Several hours later, Monica and Marnie cleared the table, rinsing out wine glasses and placing them in the dishwasher. Percy and Siobhan had said their goodbyes earlier; Marnie was spending the night. "Want to watch a movie. Eat some popcorn. I can open up my special arsenal of rom-coms. You pick. Brad Pitt. George Clooney, Denzel Washington. I know you like that guy, Benjamin Bratt. I've got him in some *Law & Order* reruns. On the other hand, we can even go way back like Sinatra, Rock Hudson, Brando, Newman, Alain Delon, and James Dean. Young, old, you name 'em, I got 'em." Monica winked. Marnie was too quiet during dinner and this worried her closest friend.

Marnie chuckled a bit. "You know I'm a John Malkovich kind of girl. That's okay. Think I'll head up to bed. No need to get all hot and bothered just to sleep alone." She slowly smiled again.

"Monica," Marnie said.

"Yes, sweetie," her friend replied.

"Thanks," Marnie said. "I'm gonna be fine."

She would be. Several days later, Jeremy and Marnie sat on her couch as she shared the story of Big and Lil' Ed with him. Unlike the talk with the Seminary Sisters, Marnie didn't cry this time. She was, in fact, unusually stoic. This time, she remembered the barrage of epitaphs Big Ed spat during her failed attempts to open the scorched door. The more Big Ed cursed her, the more her hands trembled. Why couldn't she open that door? "Marnie, you know that the impact combined with the heat from the fire probably fused the metal?" Jeremy explained. Marnie sighed.

After the accident, the emergency room doctor and later a psychologist had warned Marnie that the nature of her trauma might cause selective amnesia, but she had not taken their words seriously until new memories and emotional wounds emerged during her description of the roadside event to Jeremy. Maybe the doctors had been right that, over time, Marnie could expect to regain her full memory about the experience. Only time would tell.

After she uttered her final thought to Jeremy, they sat together on the couch for a long time. Jeremy didn't utter another word, but simply cradled Marnie all night — definitely a keeper. Marnie didn't exactly know their fate, but one thing was sure: she wanted Jeremy to be more than a "special friend" as her mother had suggested. She had meant well, but her mother was wrong on this account. Marnie wanted to share much more than clandestine, scheduled encounters with this quiet giant. Jeremey had made it clear that he was ready for more. Now it was up to Marnie to begin to address those scars as well.

Conclusion:

Sunning in the Sunny

Sunshine

As scheduled, Marnie met with the other candidates two hours early in the basement of the church where the ordination services would take place. The group had whittled down to six — Marnie, Clara, Joe Lewis, Bonita, Keith, and Hosea. Marnie's eyes light up when she saw Clara, but her heart sank to learn that Janie and Frank weren't in the number. Even Rodney was noticeably absent. Clara said that he decided to wait and try again later. Marnie heard differently: that despite his family's influence, the Governing Board felt he needed more time to mature spiritually. He and Clara were no longer dating either, but Clara seemed oddly at peace with it. Ordination was still no guarantee. However, at least Marnie could *see* the proverbial finish line. One way or another, after that night, she would know.

The ordination process was rich with pomp and circumstance. The Governing Board donned ornate purple velvet robes and family, friends, well-wishers, and some people who were curious about the potential outcome packed the church. Ordinations didn't take place annually, only when churches in the region had a sufficient number of acceptable candidates. Marnie knew that if she weren't ordained that night it might be several years before another opportunity presented itself. Tonight was her night! She believed it! She'd come so far. The entire group had. They fought the good fight and were about to finish the course. As the six candidates sat motionless in the dimly lit room, their minds jolted into the present by the abrupt entrance of the Governing Board, escorted by Reverend Joel Lowery, pastor of the host church. The group sat down at the two tables in front of the candidates.

Pastor Lowery said, "Welcome Governing Board and candidates to the final session before the ordination ceremony. I commend each candidate for reaching this point in the process." He gave a short prayer over the pending event.

The chairperson of the board, Bishop Parker Lowman, stood, prayed, and addressed the harried candidates. "This is the last test to determine which of you will be ordained. We can't tell you how proud we are that each of you made it this far. Many of your colleagues who began with you are no longer in the number. That is as it should be. Many are called, but few are chosen. God bless you." Marnie swallowed hard, but her throat remained parched.

Dr. Shelby Lewis continued. "It is our prayer that those of you who are selected for this honor will commit yourselves to this great calling and give your lives freely and sacrificially to the world. It is also our hope that if you are not selected, you will persevere, plan, and prepare to meet us again in the future." She gave the group a quick reassuring nod.

Pastor Maxwell Jepson explained the instructions. "Each of you will pull three questions from this basket, one question per round. Some of the questions are from prior assignments, discussions, and tests. However, some of them are new queries that a well-prepared candidate can answer. Only those candidates who correctly and thoughtfully answer all three of their questions will be ordained." Marnie prayed for clarity, confidence, and divine wisdom for herself and her friends. All the candidates would be present to hear each other's responses. Marnie was relieved because over the course of their training, the group had become thick as thieves. They would provide each other with moral support.

Marnie looked down at her first question. It required her to compare and contrast God's perfect will and God's permissive will as well as provide scriptures and one practical example of each. *Yes! Hallelujah!* When her turn came to respond, Marnie stumbled a bit at first, but regained her composure and provided a thoughtful and comprehensive response. Her classmates also completed the first round without much ado.

She noticed that the second round of questions were markedly more difficult. She prayed as Clara worked her way through a response about the theology of the woman at the well. Several possible schools of thought existed; Clara's response was on point. Something became clear to everyone present that

Marnie had realized much earlier. Although quiet and unassuming, Clara was the most prepared, most gifted, and probably most committed trainee in the bunch. She would soar in ministry. Although Marnie answered her second question well, Keith wasn't as fortunate. His answer was cursory at best. Marnie's heart sank, but she prayed that the Governing Board would be lenient on him.

For the third round, Marnie's question required her to discuss the nature of Jesus's encounter with the man possessed with the legion of demons. This question never came up during any of their assignments or training sessions. This was the elimination round! Marnie wiped a dribble of sweat from her forehead. She thought for a few moments, cleared her throat, and responded. After stating where the story was located in both Mark 5:6-13 and Luke 8:26-33, Marnie discussed the significance of Christ, the giver of life, entering the tombs, a place of death. She then explained the symbolism associated with the spiritually and physically bound man and Christ's ability to provide various forms of freedom. Marnie also addressed the theological debate about the presence of pigs in a Jewish area given that Jews considered such animals unclean. Finally, the anxious preacher described why the story was a miracle as she compared and contrasted the unique Markan and Lucan foci.

When she finished, Marnie tried to search the eyes of the board members. They remained stone-faced, but several nodded and scribbled on their notepads. Clara squeezed her hand when she returned to her seat, so Marnie knew that she'd done well. After each trainee answered the last question, the board exited the room, leaving the terrified trainees alone again. No one said a word. Finally, Clara stuttered, "I pray that we all make it." Everyone nodded in agreement and hugged, but no one uttered another sound. After what seemed like hours, Pastor Lowery reentered the room and beckoned the group to follow him. They led each candidate to a separate smaller room along a long narrow hall. When Marnie entered her assigned room, Pastor Lewis was waiting to embrace her.

"How excellent you are, Minister Marnie Hunter! You have done an exemplary job during this entire training process. Your loving spirit, keen intelligence, dedication to the process, sincere desire to serve, and uncompromising character, have impressed us all. Truly, God is with you. You are committed to service to God and others. It is my great pleasure to inform you that you will be ordained tonight!" Marnie heard the words that she yearned to hear for so long, but they reached her ears in slow motion. She almost couldn't believe it! She did a frenzied happy dance in her head, but only smiled faintly, nodded, and returned the congratulatory hug.

"We only have a few minutes to prepare before the group reconvenes and marches upstairs to begin the formal ordination ceremony," Pastor Lewis explained. Marnie gasped when handed the ornately adorned purple robe flecked with gold thread and beading on the collar and sleeves. It was the most beautiful garment she'd ever seen! "This is your robe now, Marnie. Wear it proudly, knowing that this is the final step in a man-made process, but that God ordained you from the beginning." Pastor Lewis' eyes sparkled.

"Thank you. Thank you. Thank you so very much, Rev. Lewis!" Marnie blushed as she realized she was gushing. "Thank you so much," she repeated as she rubbed the soft velvet on the sleeves and nap of the decorative vestment. Zipping up her new robe, Marnie scampered behind the female trailblazer into the hall, still in a state of wonderment. Yet her elation was short-lived when she realized that only four of her classmates were waiting in the line. Keith was noticeably absent. Marnie's eyes lowered as she pushed back tears.

Reverend Lewis sensed their concerns. "Please don't lose sight of your singular accomplishment! This is a time of celebration for each of you! All things come in due time — in due time." She hugged each minister and took her place at the front of the line. The Governing Board, followed by the five trainees, marched regally into the upper sanctuary. The former group took their places in the pulpit and the latter on the front, center row of the sanctuary. Marnie caught a glimpse of her parents, siblings, Jeremy, and the Seminary Sisters sitting together in a series of pews. Pastor Donaldson was there as well. *I wouldn't have made it without them.*

Despite the lengthy oral examination, the actual ordination ceremony was unusually brief. The choir sang a hymn and *The Lord's Prayer*, then a cleric read an Old and New Testament passage and a psalm. Matthew 28:18-20 reminded and encouraged the new ministers about their call to teaching, discipleship, and evangelizing. Romans 10:13-15 emphasized the importance of preachers. Pastor Lowery welcomed the congregation and gave encouraging remarks to the candidates. Bishop Lowman charged the candidates to stand and repeat a litany. He then prayed for their futures as servants of God and humanity.

The Governing Board called each candidate onto the platform separately where they surrounded him or her, placed one hand on their shoulders, and collectively prayed for them. The final phase was much like a graduation service. They called each candidate's name, but now using the title "Reverend" rather than "Minister." Each received an engraved commemorative bible trimmed in purple velvet. Finally, the new reverends were photographed individually and as a group with the Governing Board. *Reverend Marnie Hunter.* She would never forget the sound of that phrase. The choir rendered a rousing congregational song and Bishop Lowman ended the ceremony with an uplifting, encouraging prayer.

It was only after Marnie stood chatting with her family and friends at the reception that she finally realized the truth. She did it! In retrospect, the ordination process never felt like a weight on her shoulders, but rather a mysterious challenge she felt compelled to complete. "I am so very proud of you, *Reverend Hunter.*" Her father gave her one of his famous bear hugs. Marnie could tell that her mother had been crying. The two women kissed and held each other for a long time. After a series of similar embraces with each member of her family and friendship circle, Marnie excused herself and rushed to congratulate her peers.

Tears flowed down Clara's cheeks as they swayed back-and-forth in a warm hug. "We did it! We did it!" said Clara in a clear, confident, certain voice that

Marnie hadn't heard before. "I will never forget you, Marnie," promised Clara.

"Nor I you," responded Marnie.

"I promise to let you know as soon as I get my church assignment. Guess what! Pastor Lewis volunteered to mentor me!" Clara said. Marnie was pleased.

"Friends for life!" said Marnie.

"Yes, friends for life!" echoed Clara. After another long hug, both women returned to their respective parties. Marnie felt a soft tap on her right shoulder and turned to find Pastor Donaldson beaming.

"Well, well. I guess I will have to call you Reverend from now on." He chuckled.

"Only for the next month," she quipped.

"I will be very pleased to do so," he said. Marnie believed him.

"I don't want to keep you from your family and friends. I just wanted to say how proud I am of you and excited about this great accomplishment. You will surely have many opportunities as an ordained minister. I hope that you will consider staying on at Bethlehem a little while longer. We really need you. I really need you."

"Thank you for your kind words and the invitation, Pastor Donaldson. Who knows what the future holds? I just want to cherish tonight a little while longer," she said. He nodded and moved back into the crowd. An unknown woman interrupted her trek back to her circle of support. Dressed in a conservative blue suit, she extended her right hand toward the newly ordained minister.

"Congratulations, Reverend Hunter. I am so very happy about your great accomplishment tonight. I know from personal experience how daunting the preparation can be." Marnie could feel the warmth in her words. "I'm Rev. Dr. Beverly Lancaster."

"Thank you, Rev. Dr. Lancaster." Curiosity was getting the best of Marnie. "So you're a minister as well? Are you a pastor?"

"Please call me Beverly. I was ordained about fifteen years ago in the northern district. It's been a while, but it's an experience you will never forget. I was then a pastor for about five years before taking a position as editor of the denomination's publishing board. I started writing in my teens and wrote my first book in my early twenties. I've been writing ever since. When the post on the board became available, I was a bit torn to leave the pastorate, but it was the best decision I ever made. That's why I wished to attend your ordination." The woman's lips curled up in a smile.

"Thank you for coming," said Marnie. "It's an honor to meet a reverend who has taken a different path as God's servant. It's especially wonderful to meet a female reverend."

Dr. Lancaster nodded and her lips curled even higher. "Yes, there are so many paths we can take to serve God. I don't want to take up too much of your time. You should savor this experience with your loved ones. However, I wanted to notify you personally that the publishing house is extremely interested in your book proposal on female clerics. It successfully passed the first round of reviews and we want to read more. Have you written any chapters?" With all the hubbub around the ordination as well as her hectic work schedule, Marnie almost forgot about that book proposal. She submitted it on a fluke and had no idea it would spur any interest.

"I can't believe it!" Marnie squashed the impulse to jump up and down. "Oh my, I can't believe this! Yes. Yes. I have written four of the seven chapters. I would be happy to send them to you. When would you like to get them? Where should I mail them?" Marnie rambled.

"Rev. Hunter, send them directly to me. ASAP. Here's my business card." They shook hands again as Marnie promised to put the chapters in the mail the next day. "Congratulations again, I look forward to receipt of the chapters." Dr. Lancaster moved toward the front door. Marnie the author. Maybe her pipedream would become a reality. *God is good!* Marnie walked back over to her family and friends but hesitated to enter the circle. She glanced around at each of them and thanked God for her blessings. She would tell them about the book possibility later.

"Well, what's next for Reverend Marnie Hunter?" She turned to see the Seminary Sisters posed in front of her. They chattered over each other as they inspected her new bible and caressed the folds of her robe.

"Where can I buy me one of these blinged-out robes?" Percy methodically scrutinized the details on Marnie's vestment.

"Marnie and I know how you can get one free!" Monica's eyes sparkled. Marnie just winked. Percy rolled her eyes and shook her head from side to side.

"We have something special planned for you next week," teased Siobhan.

"Oh no. Now I'm really afraid!" Marnie winked. They all laughed and closed the circle of hugs around Marnie one more time.

Jeremy hugged Marnie in the receiving line, but purposely avoided entering the congratulatory circles that continually opened and closed around his girlfriend. Marnie didn't question his behavior; she noticed his eyes fixed on her each time she looked in his direction. They both knew that they would have their own special quiet time later that night.

Several weeks passed and Marnie sat at her favorite restaurant with her favorite girlfriends. She told them about her book deal for *Women Warriors*. She already celebrated the news with her family and Jeremy. They cheered aloud and lifted their glasses of tea in a toast.

Percy's head leaned back in laughter. "Marnie, you're a unicorn. Your life is like a Hollywood movie. Who knows what will happen next. I'm just glad I get to hang around to see it."

"Same here. Reverend Hunter is on her way up," Siobhan echoed. Monica only nodded and winked.

"A movie about me, really? That's hilarious." Marnie's eyebrows raised, but she decided to play along. "So who would play me in the movie? Angelina Jolie, Jessica Chastain, or Jennifer Aniston, pray tell?" Marnie rolled her eyes upward and pressed her right pointer finger at the side of her lips.

Monica interjected. "Who would play you, Marnie? Maybe someone like Maggie Gyllenhaal or Michelle Williams. Cerebral types. Or maybe a younger version of Meryl Streep. I think she has a daughter."

"Heck no! They're all impressive, but none of them will do," challenged Percy. The three women paused, gazed at each other, and as if by telepathy chimed in unison, "Lupita Nyong'o!"

Their celebration continued for several hours. Passersby grinned at the infectious interactions between the longtime, somewhat weatherworn, but optimistic friends. Their raucous laughter and banter wafted up into the night sky.

Prologue

Marnie methodically stepped into the foyer of her condominium, dropped her keys on the table, kicked off her shoes, and plopped down on the deep sofa. Today was a good day — a very good day. She noticed the red flicking button on her answering machine an arm's length away. Despite technological advances, Marnie still used the tried-and-true device. Eyes closed, she pressed the furiously blinking button. A small voice rose above the static. "I think this is the right number. This message is for Minister Marnie Hunter. I hope you remember me. This is Edward Fountain. You know, Lil' Ed... Please Miss Marnie, I need your help!"